The Last Fay

The Last Fay
or, The New Marvelous Lamp

by
Honoré de Balzac

Translated, annotated and introduced by
Brian Stableford

A Black Coat Press Book

ISBN 978-1-61227-547-5. First Printing. August 2016. Published by Black Coat Press, an imprint of Hollywood Comics.com, LLC, P.O. Box 17270, Encino, CA 91416.

Introduction

La Dernière fée, ou La Nouvelle Lampe merveilleuse, here translated as *The Last Fay; or, The New Marvelous Lamp*, was originally published in two volumes in Paris in 1823 bearing the signature "M. Horace de Saint-Aubin," a pseudonym under which Honoré de Balzac (1799-1850) had already issued four other novels. That edition was credited to a consortium of three booksellers and a printer, but it is believed that the author paid for its printing himself. The novel was reissued in three volumes, in a slightiy revised version, by Delongchamps in 1825.

As with all of Balzac's early pseudonymous novels save one—*Wann Chlore, ou la Prédestination* (1825), which he rewrote as *Jane la pâle* (1836)—Balzac subsequently disowned it, and it was not until the various editions of his collected works were published after his death that it was added to his recognized canon. Balzac claimed that he had eliminated his early novels from the list of his acknowledged works because they were "collaborations," and numerous subsequent critics have taken the view that they ought to be regarded as hackwork, but if that was true of any of them, it was surely not the case with *La Dernière fée*, which the author took some trouble to get into print in spite of the apparent initial indifference of contemporary publishers.

At least some of those early works are probably better considered as experiments that the author subsequently considered to have failed, and thus wanted to discard, especially if they did not fit into the vast cross-sectional patchwork study of contemporary French society that he called *La Comédie humaine*, which he regarded as the core of his endeavor. He was probably right about their relative failure, but it does not follow from that assessment that they ought to have been buried and forgotten, because failed experiments can often be interesting and educational; that is particularly true of literary experiments that are not only attempting to test an author's individual capabilities, but are trying to test the capabilities of prose fiction itself, in terms to what might potentially be done with it and how.

In the early 1820s, when Balzac published his various pseudonymous works—some under other names than Horace de St. Aubin—the French Romantic Movement was just beginning to take wing; its leading writers were only just beginning to define themselves as a movement, which initially coalesced around the *cénacle* founded by Charles Nodier, when he became the librarian at the Bibliothèque de l'Arsenal in 1824. Balzac was not a regular participant Nodier's cénacle, but he was acquainted with many of the writers who were, and subsequently attended some of the other salons associated with the movement, as well as having an overlapping coterie of his own. One of the works that must have helped to prompt Balzac to write *La Dernière fée* is Nodier's *Trilby, ou le lutin d'Argail* (1822; tr. as *Trilby*)[1], which was itself partly inspired by the fact that leading members of the German Romantic Movement had adopted a radically new attitude to *märchen* (folktales), in which they hoped to find the essential *volksgeist* (folk-spirit) of the German-speaking peoples,

---

[1] Available from Black Coat Press, ISBN 978-1-61227-455-3/

and had begun writing sophisticated *kunstmärchen* (art-folktales) in some profusion.

Germany was still fragmented at the beginning of the nineteenth century, and its consolidation as a modern nation-state was severely disrupted by the Napoleonic Wars, whereas France had achieved a much greater degree of unity and national solidity more than a century earlier. There was, in consequence, no incentive for the French Romantics to hunt for an native equivalent of the German *volksgeist*, and French writers had, in any case, been dabbling with materials akin to those of German *kunstmärchen* for a long time, ever since a vogue for composing imitation folktales had taken hold in the literary salons associated with Louis XIV's court and had spawned an entire tradition of fantastic fiction, whose recognized figurehead was Madame d'Aulnoy.

That tradition had a kind of standard reference work in *Le Cabinet des fées, ou Collection choisie de contes de fées et autres contes merveilleux* [The Showcase of Fays: A Selected Collection of Tales of Enchantment and other marvelous tales]. The first part of the title was initially used on a reissue of Madame d'Aulnoy's stories published in 1717, but the version with which Balzac was presumably acquainted, and which seems to be the one featured in the novel, was a plush 41-volume set published in Amsterdam between 1785 and 1789, assembled by the Chevalier Charles-Joseph de Mayer, each volume of which was illustrated by engravings made under the direction of Nicolas Delaunay from drawings by Clement-Pierre Marillier. That definitive *Cabinet des fées* added to the collected works of Madame d'Aulnoy stories by her fellow salon writers, the derivative works of Charles Perrault—which were more ostentatiously adapted for the simultaneous entertainment and *civilization* [moral education] of children—and, most importantly, the most popular stories taken from Antoine Galland's *Les Mille et une nuits* (tr. as The Arabian Nights), which claimed, dubiously in some instances, to be translated from Arabic. That fusion of materials created a syncretic genre in which the *"fées"* employed by Madame d'Aulnoy and her peers were mingled and confused with the *"génies"* abundantly featured by Galland. Mayer's collection was also carefully bowdlerized to remove much of the erotic material featured in the "original" stories, thus establishing the definitive *Cabinet des fées* as a work not only fit for children but fit to provide the backbone of their literary education.

Given that background, it is inevitable that the French Romantic writers who adopted an interest in mock-folkloristic fiction adopted an attitude to that material markedly different from that of their German counterparts, considerably livelier in tone and manner, although by no means devoid of seriousness. The blithely playful *Trilby*, about a *lutin* (goblin or brownie) benevolently smitten with a Scottish housewife, is a cardinal example of that variant attitude. Balzac also began writing in a period when similarly playful stage adaptations of materials from the *Cabinet des fées*—the ancestors of modern pantomimes—were enjoying something of a vogue in Paris, and one reference in his story strongly suggests that he had seen the comic opera *La Petite lampe merveilleuse* [The Marvelous Little Lamp] (1822), with music by Alexandre Piccinni and a libretto by Eugène Scribe, the key motif of which is reproduced and transfigured in *La Dernière fée*.

In the context of those contemporary works, *La Dernière fée* is, in effect, Balzac's attempt to join with a popular game, but it is also, to some extent, a reaction against it. The project is obviously an attempt to take up an existing thread, but to twist it in a new direction and to form and entirely new knot: to deploy popular mock-folkoristic materials in a novel way, more advanced in both literary and philosophical terms than the sophistications already added by generations of French writers over the past century. All of those sophistications had, in one way or another, attempted to introduce a certain dose of "realism"—or cynicism—into the fantastic backcloth provided by the tales, challenging their seeming naivety with deft irony, but Balzac wanted to alter that dose, both quantitatively and qualitatively, in order to produce a new alloy, as he was later to do in some of the "philosophical studies" that formed the most eccentric section of *La Comédie humaine*. The narrative strategy of *La Dernière fée* is markedly different from that of the author's later fantasy of wish-granting. *La Peau de Chagrin* (1831; tr. under various titles, including *The Magic Skin*) and there is no doubt that the narrative strategy of the latter novel is far more successful, but the earlier one is interesting not as a kind of preliminary sketch, but as an alternative approach to the problem.

It is impossible to discuss that narrative strategy in detail at this point without introducing spoilers that would undermine the dramatic tension of the story, so I shall add a further comment on what the author achieved—partially, at least—in an afterword. In terms of introducing the novel, however, it is important to note that a difference in their attitude to mock-folkloristic materials was not the only thing that distinguished French writers associated with the Romantic Movement from German ones. The French Movement also took aboard a powerful specific influence from Jean-Jacques Rousseau, who was the primary domestic inspiration of

9

the writer and critic who gave French Romanticism its name and definition, Madame de Staël.

Rousseau's influence was particularly strong in respect of his famous argument that humans were once naturally virtuous, and only became vicious because of the deleterious effects of civilization; the literary figuration and analysis of various exemplars of the Rousseauesque unspoiled "Child of Nature" is very prolific in Romantic writings, some offered in earnest support of the philosopher's controversial allegation, some in scathing demolition of it, and some in a spirit of inquisitive ambiguity. The first great prose classic of the French Movement, François-René de Châteaubriand's *Atala* (1801) was an intended criticism that many readers misinterpreted as a celebration. The hero of *La Dernière fée* is Balzac's version of a Child of Nature, and is just as distinctive and idiosyncratic as the story's treatment of materials borrowed from the *Cabinet des fées*. Indeed, the fact that Balzac's Child of Nature is selectively "civilized" by tales explicitly designed for the *civilization* of children, rather than by the social forces of literal civilization that Rousseau thought deleterious, is the central irony of the story.

When seen in the context of French Romantic fiction, therefore, and as a contribution to the evolution of modern fantastic fiction, *La Derniere fée* is by no means a negligible work, and it still bears an interesting relationship to the genre of modern fantasy that has flourished in Britain, America in France in the last forty years. In the context of that modern fantasy genre there has been a new boom in the production of transfigurative works reprocessing the materials of the *Cabinet des fées*, and the genre has also claimed and taken aboard numerous recent exemplars of the Child of Nature, most famously and most strikingly Edgar Rice Burroughs' Tarzan.

The *Cabinet des fées*, and the genre that it helped to define, has always been cursed by problems of translation rising from the confusion and reconfiguration of once-distinct sets of hypothetical beings associated with the folklore of different societies. Madame d'Aulnoy's description of *"contes de fées"* was translated into English as "fairy stories," although the French *féerie* mans "enchantment" and *fées* are, strictly speaking, enchantresses (as in the Arthurian Morgan le Fay). The English term "fairy" can relate to various folkloristic figures, including Teutonic elves, but the term was given a crucial literary figuration in Elizabethan times by William Shakespeare and Edmund Spenser, particularly the former's characterization of the fairies of *A Midsummer Night's Dream*, which exerted an enormous influence on subsequent literary and artistic imagery. Although some confusion between Shakespearean fairies and French *fées* is evident in the *Cabinet des fées*, and is thus carried forward into much nineteenth-century mock-folkloristic fiction, there is a certain awkwardness about the conventional translation, and I prefer the translation "fays," which I have employed in the present text.

Confusions also arise because of Galland's use of the term "génie" [genius], which is usually transcribed directly, and neologistically, in English versions of his stories and their derivatives as "genie" instead of being translated. Galland was, however, translating the Arabic word *djinni*, whose plural is *djinn*, and it is arguable that the supposed similarity between Arabic *djinn* and French *génies* is even more problematic than that between French *fées* and English fairies. Again, I have elected to emphasize the problematic features of the syncretic genre by translating Balzac's *génie* and *génies* not as genie and genies but as djinni and djinn. This might seem disconcerting, but it does help to emphasize the calculated impropriety of Balzac's idiosyncratic representation of the supposed relationship between *génies* and *enchanteurs* [enchanters] in the Empire of the Fays, which makes the hypothetical species comprised by the two categories into a masculine equivalent of *fees*; the logic of the author's decision to do that will eventually become manifest to readers within the story.

This translation was made from the London Library's copy of the 1963 facsimile of the 1823 edition published in Paris by Les Bibliophile de l'Originale. Comparative reference was also made version of the 1976 Slatkine facsimile reprint of the 1825 edition reproduced on the Bibliothèque Nationale's *gallica* website. It is arguable that the latter text ought to be regarded as the definitive one by virtue of having been revised, but the amendments are mostly trivial and do not seem to me to constitute significant improvements; I have therefore preferred the earlier version.

Brian Stableford

Chapter I
The Chemist

There was once a chemist and his wife who lived happily together; the husband loved crucibles, and the wife cherished retorts, from which it followed that they had the most agreeable life possible. With his spectacles wedged on his nose, the chemist was always occupied watching his flasks boil, sometimes stimulating the fire with an old bellows; he did not say a word, and his wife, sitting in the laboratory, did not complain about the smoke, the charcoal or the odor; she did not speak any more than her husband, for her only language was the amiable smile that she made to wander over her naïve lips when, fatigued by his work, he decided to dart a glance at his cherished wife. She was a beautiful woman, and he was a handsome man, but as they stayed in their laboratory all day, and did not look at one another often, and as they adored one another and scarcely thought about their appearance, you might not have perceived their beauty at first.

The laboratory where they lived resembled a cellar; the walls could have rendered thirty quintals of soot if anyone had cared to clean them. The glass in the window, which was almost ogival, with small panes retained by lead, had achieved a veto over the daylight, which it almost prevented from passing through, so thick with dust was it; but outside, a joyful vine played elegantly. The tiled floor, always damp and dirty, offered singular aspects; here and there, a neat circle or square was perceptible, like a newly-minted coin, because a physical object had remained there for some time.

Finally, it was legible in the furrows of the dust imprinted by the broom how rarely a generous hand had desired to bring order to the chaos. One might have imagined that the spiders had lived so long in peace that they had assembled one day to make a constitution, but that they had stopped at the clause that would have granted individual liberty to flies; the voice of a cricket was often audible, rejoicing in not being troubled in its shelter by interference; and more than one mouse ran around tranquilly in that abode of innocence, peace and chemistry, without fear of sword-thrusts or baited traps.

In the middle of that mass of tables, bottles and instruments, the chemist, his hair covered with the white ash of his charcoal, pored over a retort, and the fire cast its ruddy reflection over everything that surrounded him, which faded away over the chemist's wife, who was alternately working and looking at the interior with a satisfied expression. The black vault, the absence of sunlight—which only showed itself in the space left between the door and the window—the chemical apparatus and the chemist husband would not have pleased everyone, but since the chemist and his wife were happy, no one ought to criticize them, for people might think that happiness depends on a thrust of the broom, the death of a cricket, a spider's web or the tail of a poor mouse, but it actually depends on something else entirely.

One morning in spring, a window had been opened; pure air was circulating and the sun, sending one of its most beautiful rays into the laboratory, was tracing a bright line, in which a multitude of little motes of dust were floating, which seemed to be running after one another like swarms of flies about a steam on a beautiful summer evening. The cricket that had been crying like a cantor at the funeral of a village seigneur met a female cricket and shut up; the mouse went back to its hole with a rat; and, the gentle influence of the air penetrating the chemist, he looked at his wife.

She was sitting in a worm-eaten armchair, amusing herself contemplating, for the thousandth time, the illustrations in the *Cabinet des fées*; her ingenuousness was painted on her face, her pale golden hair, arranged in a maidenly manner, added to a radiance of innocence in her blue eyes, devoid of malice. She divined that her husband was looking at her, and abandoned her book to look at her spouse. The chemist reflected, in the midst of the silence, that the young woman that he had taken merely to refresh his eyes during his long toil might have become something other than something to look at.

It cost him a great many test tubes to find out, he broke more than one bottle and the peace of the laboratory was troubled for the first time in five years. The chemist spilled I don't know how many ingredients, and his fire went out. The chemist's wife, like Psyche receiving the first kiss of Amour, said nothing. A few months later, however, she screamed so loudly that it was audible for a quarter of a league around, and terror reigned in the nearby village—you shall know why in due course. In short, those screams were motivated by the coming into the world of a child as beautiful as the day.

The laboratory was henceforth witness to the most charming scenes; the black vault resounded with infantile cries, and the chemist had no complaint to make about it. Caliban, quitting the spade, came to look through the window, trying to make his horrible coarse face smile, and adopting a pretty voice to speak to the child. The chemist's wife, still sitting in her worm-eaten armchair, bounced the brat on her knees, covering him with kisses as soon as he smiled. She excited his laughter, and if he broke a test tube the chemist laughed, saying that he had already been the cause of the loss of more than one.

The wife that the chemist had married for her naivety and the limited extent of her knowledge deployed all her soul over her child, and became intelligent regarding everything that concerned him; she lived on the breath of the little being that played on her bosom, after having extracted therefrom a milk as pure as his mother's soul, and the blissful chemist perceived that nature had crucibles more beautiful than his and a method of combining mixtures far superior to his.

That chemist was one of the most astonishing and original minds that the sun's fire had ever warned. If ideas depend on the interior form of the brain, his own must have had the bizarre aspect of the chemical products that apothecaries expose to the curiosity of passersby, and which present such brilliant crystallizations. Since his childhood, he had only lived for the arts and had done nothing but study the natural sciences with ardor. Thus, he had such a profound and solid knowledge of human nature that, to begin with, he had, as we have just seen, a child; but afterwards, he succeeded in knowing the physical mechanisms of our machine so well that merely by visual examination he could discover the symptoms, the progress and the cause of a malady, and cure it rapidly and painlessly.

That perfection of science did not only relate to the body; It was applied to the soul, and he knew the cause of our pains and our pleasures, our passions and our virtues, with such a superiority that, first of all, he and his wife had attained the perfection of happiness and their marriage was as pure as the African sky; but thereafter he suddenly knew what such and such a man needed in order to be happy, after having examined him briefly; as soon as he had palpated the head, the foot and the spine, he could tell him what he ought to do, and even to say, in a given social situation.

What proves his extreme wisdom and the sublimity of his mind is that, having reached the summit of human science, he lived in his laboratory, with a cricket, a mouse, Caliban, a few spiders, his wife and his child. To be sure, the chemist could have gone to Paris, where he would have amassed as much glory as a hundred thousand men, but he had reflected and had seen:

That if he cured everyone, everyone would come to him, that there would not have been any more sick people, and hence no more physicians, and that the physicians would then have invited him to pass into the third hemisphere;

That, divining all interests, he would have accommodated all legal disputes, and that, the lawyers imitating the doctors, his science would cause him to run the risk of falling into the hands of prosecutors—for he cut the questioning short—even crueler than physicians;

That if the government learned that he could make diamonds, he would be locked up like the donkey in "Peau-d'âne" in order to make diamonds perpetually,[2] or his eyes might be put out, or some similar step taken, to prevent him from doing it—and in either case, he would find governments even crueler than doctors and lawyers;

---

[2] "Peau d'âne" (1697; tr. as "Donkeyskin") is one of the initial set of Perrault's tales, the richest in strange sexual symbolism; the donkey whose skin is adopted after its death as a disguise by the heroine has the useful ability to shit gold.

That, finally, the perfectibility of human reason would become the ruination of society, which only exists because of everyone's follies, maladies, stupidities, passions, itches and taxes.

Then, he had had the incredible rationality to compare the glory he would have acquired with the smoke of his furnace; wealth with the charcoal that blackened his hands and whose vapor would end up killing him; and, seizing the god of happiness by the ears, he made it his task never to let him go, by never leaving his cottage.

It was thus that he simplified his existence. To give himself an occupation, he tried to discover new secrets, took a pretty wife who did nothing, knew nothing and hardly spoke, and an idiotic domestic, and decreed that for all of them, nature began at the cabin door and finished at the garden wall.

In the evening, they went out for a stroll along a covered pathway, admired the pure air of the sky; the chemist complimented Caliban on the appearance of the garden, and he compared the mysterious light of the stars to the amorous gleam in his wife's eyes. She smiled in thinking that she was as beautiful as a star, and she adored her husband; Caliban admired the fact that they had so much intelligence—and they went back to their cottage, happy and content, laughing at other people, whom the chemist depicted to them frantically trying to capture soap-bubbles that burst in their hands. And the three individuals made their way in life, as healthy as sturdy oaks, seeing a rose in each of their smiles, a bouquet in every thought, and a pearl in every speech, having no time to desire because they worked all day and slept all night: happy, a thousand times happy!

In that regard, the chemist, clapping his hands and depositing a kiss on the lips of his wife—who thought that all men were chemists—applauded his decision, and thought that he had solved the greatest problem of all, that of a happy life.

From then on, he stirred his crucibles more and more, sought with an unparalleled ardor to steal one secret more from nature, and tried to explain to his wife what he was doing. She did not understand any of it, but she listened attentively, as if she understood something, for she would have given all the sciences for a smile for her little Abel, and all the ducal crowns in Europe for a word from her husband.

Those three individuals has no communication with the rest of creation, and that needs proof; for that, it is necessary to go back into their past life and explain how they came to be living in such profound retreat.

Adjacent to their cottage flourished a garden that seemed made expressly for them; vegetables took pleasure in growing there, the trellis buckled under the grapes, and a pure and limpid spring watered that little corner of the promised land. The chemist, whose wife believed everything that her husband said—if he had claimed that it was day in the middle of a winter night she would have replied that she could see the sun—had proved to her that in only eating vegetables, the passions were less ardent and the intelligence keener, so they lived on the produce of that terrain, where two chickens found their nourishment and a cow its fresh grass.

Caliban, the domestic of that fortunate household, gathered the grapes and the harvest, milled the grain by means of a machine invented by the chemist, and knew no other existence than getting up in the morning, cultivating the garden, eating soberly, preparing the chemist's meals, spinning in winter, making cloth and going to bed; furthermore, he had suppressed usage of thought as something too fatiguing, and the *nec plus ultra* of his employment was going to pay the tax-collector of the commune the seventeen francs that the chemist owed annually for his two arpents of land, his wife, his chickens, his cricket, his mouse, his spiders, Caliban, the cow, the brat, the rat and a poor black dog that was the friend of the entire household. Thus, the French government assembled the two Chambres, equipped the conscripts with their rifles, uniforms, captain, colonel, chief of general staff and almoner, all to give assistance and protection to its seven immense ministries and its colossal administration of fourteen things, for a modest sum of seventeen francs! In truth, how can one complain about the burden of taxes?

The cottage in which they lived...what do I see? Great God, twenty-five pages! Times are so hard that no one will ever read a longer chapter.

Chapter II
The Chemist's Opinions

The cottage in which those four individuals made for one another lived (this is the continuation of the proof of their isolation) merits an exact description, for one cannot put too much verity into a fairy tale; then, at least, if the basis is false, the details are true. So, you should know that the happy cottage was situated twenty leagues from Paris, in one of those valleys to which nature seems to have retreated with all her treasures. There were the most picturesque situations, the most elegant trees, the most cheerful meadows, the freshness of limpid streams, a hanging vine, a mill and its sonorous cascade, and, in the midst of that landscape, more than one young woman singing without cadence in her pure voice. Thus, the echo of the songs in question, which mingled with the sounds of the herdsman's pastoral flute, added to the delights of nature the charm of melancholy, which only ever comes from humans.

In sum, it was a valley so pleasant, so remote, and so distant from any city, that all disgraced ministers would have wanted to live there during the initial phase of their fall. The present minister will find the address at the end of the story.

As the chemist offered nothing to thieves but science books, charcoal, retorts, little bottles and ink, he had been able, without danger, to live in a cottage situated on the slope of a pretty hill, from which that enchanting view could be seen, and which was some distance from the nearby village. The chemist always left his door open, and that habit went well with the simplicity of their way of life. The cottage was placed in such a way that the chimney was on a level with the plateau of the hill, above which an immense forest commenced, from which the chemist obtained his charcoal and the precious ingredients he needed

Here it becomes urgently necessary to make an observation that will support the assertion that it is necessary to prove. Those who have traveled a little know that there are in France remote spots, little villages buried in lands far from roads, where people live in profound ignorance of things of this world, where people only learn about social revolutions from changes in the arms found printed at the top of the tax-collector's forms or the sign above the tobacconist's shop—a sign that, in parentheses, contains the history of the last twenty years written in six layers of different colors. They are villages, in sum, where those who do not pay taxes and do not take tobacco live and die without knowing who the mortal that governs them is, and will never know of the existence of oil of Macassar, Lord Byron, hydrogen gas, bell-tents, duchesses or water-carriers. That is a great misfortune for sovereigns, poets, gas-manufacturers and, most of all, duchesses, but it is the truth—and that luminous observation has no other purpose than to inform you that the village a quarter of a league from which the chemist's habitation stood was one of those fortunate villages.

That's not all! The chemist's habitation was surrounded by another *cordon sanitaire* of ignorance even more impossible to cross, which had been woven by superstition and the village beadle. To sense its force fully it is necessary to go back to the epoch of the chemist's arrival in the region.

It was night—an obscure night, for the moon was circling silently between big clouds, black in the middle and yellow-tinted at the edges. It was a Saturday, the day of the Sabbat, and the last Saturday in the month of December, the epoch of the general assembly of witches. Caliban, the bearer of a horrible face, which made him resemble an imp extracted from great cauldron no. 1, which is stirred with a red skimmer, was leading by the bridle a poor skinny nag that had the air of the one of the Apocalypse whose bones can be counted, and which carries Death.

That horse was dragging an open cart that allowed the sight of a host of mortars, retorts, scientific instruments, quadrants, globes, test tubes, telescopes, furnaces, etc., and in the bosom of that chemical cargo sat the chemist in person, his head covered by a bearskin cap, wearing spectacles, and using both hands to hold his books and his ingredients in place.

The winter wind was whistling, and more than one tree branch fell on to the thatched roofs, producing a phantasmal noise that caused the circle to tighten of those who were sitting around a somber hearth, listening to the tales of an old woman whose face resembled the rennet-apples eaten at Pentecost.

The ground, being covered in snow, did not permit the footfalls of Caliban's horse to be heard, nor the noise of the infernal cart, with the consequence that it was possible to believe, on seeing the frightful cortege pass, through poor windows full of flaws, that it was dancing in the air. The bell that was tolling at that moment for a funeral, the frightful tales of grandmothers, fear, Caliban's oaths, the whistling of the tempest, and the bloody light of the moon, which gave the spectacle the air of the devil's convoy, all contributed to sowing such terror that the man who had sold the cottage and the en-closure to the chemist—with some difficulty—washed the coins in vinegar and believed that the bonnet of Liberty was the devil's claw; he could only get anyone else to take them in the next village, to which he went for the first time in his life.

All that might not have had any consequence if the chemist had been seen thereafter behaving like a normal person, coming to market, drinking in the tavern and smoking a pipe, but no, none of that happened.

So, curiosity being the same everywhere, people went to investigate what was happening in the home of the devil's envoy. Nothing was seen coming out of his abode; everything there seemed dead, except that an abundant black smoke was swirling above the enormous chimney of his cottage—from which it was concluded that Satan had established one of Hell's ventilation-shafts there; all the more so as the chemist had enlarged his fireplace in such a fashion that a cavalier with his lance, his pennant, his horse, his carbine and his turned-up moustache could have passed into it without the cockade on his shako suffering any damage. Certainly, on seeing such a chimney always occupied in vomiting smoke, the most impassive peasant was obliged to draw sinister conclusions. Others might perhaps have been astonished if it had not smoked, but in a village, and especially an ignorant village, things proceed differently than they do elsewhere.

What brought the terror to a peak, and completed the construction of an impenetrable rampart between the cottage and the village, was the beadle's story. The latter, fortified by the sacerdotal authority that he had as a clerical instrument of the Law, chanced one evening to go to the habitation, partly because the curé desired to know whether the chemist, devilry notwithstanding, would be making the bread offering.

The beadle—an important man in the village, for he could read fluently and calculate—who had a strong mind, perceived the frightful Caliban sitting on a large stone covered in moss; he was playing with his dear black dog, which was confounding its intelligent head with that of the domestic with the turned-up nose and thick lips that allowed a glimpse of teeth like pallets. The chemist had a face as black as an oven; he was dressed grotesquely, like all busy scientists; he was caressing his long black beard with hands as slender as those of a midwife; and madame his wife, laying her pretty head brilliant with amour on her husband's shoulder, was mingling the gold of her blonde tresses with the chemist's abundant jet black hair; her pale and delicate hands, caressing her husband's beard, indicated that she wanted to prevent him from meditating, and desired a soft gaze of affection.

The setting sun spread a ruddy glow over the group, which caused the beadle to believe that the cottage was the porch of Hell. What he had been told about the temptation of Saint Anthony returned to his mind, and Caliban appeared to him as a great ape sitting on a giant tortoise; his dog was a horned demon; a stone covered in green moss was the large toad that leapt into the saint's water-jug; the chemist's beautiful wife was the pretty she-devil with the amorous hands, the celestial face and the eyes of a courtesan who wants her account settled; and, finally, the chemist seemed to him to be the chief devil surrounded by serpents, and Caliban's spade his fork. But what caused the disorder in the beadle's senses was that, when he arrived, the cricket, the chickens, the cow and the dog were crying; the chemist and his wife were laughing in bursts and Caliban was cursing, because the dog had nipped his ear.

The beadle was terrified, and fled, believing that a thousand basketfuls of devils were on his heels; he recounted everywhere that he had run the greatest dangers, and that it would be folly to go on to the hill where the chemist—or rather the Devil—lived.

In the superstitious times in which young women who had nightmares were burned, claiming that they were prey to an incubus, things had been seen no less astonishing than what the beadle reported. The ignorant village believed that individual's story, and no one any longer looked at the cottage without fear mingled with curiosity; thus, a double barrier of ignorance and dread served as a boundary wall for the village and the blissful cottage, which found itself, as we have already seen, separated from the rest of creation.

Let us therefore return to the chemist and his meek and ignorant wife, to Caliban the idiot and little Abel, the cricket, the mouse, etc,

As Abel grew older, he played with the dog, often stuck his dainty fingers into the cricket's hole, and teased the mouse, but those worthy creatures were not annoyed by that, all the more so because Abel's mother, when he caught the cricket one day, made him understand that he must not injure it. Oh, she knew what she was doing, the poor mother, when she explained to him that she would suffer if anyone hurt Abel; so the dear child said, in the tender voice of infancy: "Go, little cricket," and watched it march away, smiling angelically.

At that scene, which you might perhaps think overly naïve, the chemist quit his furnaces, allowing one of the most beautiful fluids he had ever found to evaporate, and, sitting down on a stool, played with his child as if he were a child himself; and Caliban, putting all his weight on his spade, desired a wife.

Abel was not confined in any swaddling-clothes; his delicate limbs developed in liberty; he roamed around the laboratory, making his mother shiver every time he bumped into bottles, poisons and acids, but Abel reassured her, calling in his soft voice "I'm being careful, Mother!" He tangled the thousand curls of his beautiful hair with spider's webs, smeared his face with charcoal, climbed on the furnaces, wanted to taste everything, touch everything, and laughed, frolicking without chagrin and without constraint—and nature smiled on the divine tableau that the laboratory presented, where she reigned as sovereign.

But who could describe the joy, the delight and the stamping feet of Abel when his mother, opening a volume of the *Cabinet des fées*, showed him the illustrations? He deployed all the force of his beautiful dark eyes, moist with the sap of infancy, and resembled an infant Jesus by Raphael, when, grouped around his mother, who still seemed a pure virgin, he admired the Green Serpent, Gracieuse and Percinet, the Blue Bird, and the Fay Truitonne; but the most beautiful illustration, the one that excited his ecstasy the most, was that of the Fay Abricotine.[3]

---

[3] "Serpentin vert" (tr. as "The Green Serpent"); "Gracieuse et Percinet" (tr. as "Graciosa and Percinet"), "L'Oiseau bleu" (tr. as "The Blue Bird"), which features the *fée* Truitonne, and "Le Prince Lutin" (tr. as "The Imp Prince"), which features the *fée* Abricotine, are all stories by Madame d'Aulnoy, from *Contes de fées* (1696-99), all of which were included in both the 1717 version of the *Cabinet des fées* and Mayer's expanded set.

Abel's face announced delicacy and naivety combined in a character of affection, mildness, love and courage, which would have made him, at the age of eighteen, the most handsome page that the court of a princess could ever have seen, but the chemist had plans for him that were too bizarre for him ever to be seen at a princely court.

That great man, always meditating, always seeking, had ended up by finding; his reflections told him that there were, for social human beings, far more evils than goods. He claimed that Adam and Eve had only been happy in Paradise because they had lived in ignorance, and that their depiction in the Bible shows us the way to happiness: that civilization provided, it is true, astonishing enjoyments, but that desires and troubles were as cruel there as the pleasures were exquisite. In a state of nature, therefore, one had the fewest evils, plus the ignorance of pleasures—that, in sum, one enjoyed little, but the little in question was unalloyed, like spring water.

It was that doctrine that had brought him to the cottage where his wife, Caliban and he led a life exempt from alarms, a rustic life, broad and even poetic. Love, gratitude, benevolence and light labor filled their souls, and the sweet alliance of everything that nature presets to humans, combined with the simplest sentiments, composed their code. Fruits ornamented their table; the light of the sky was theirs; pure water slaked their thirst; their clothing was modest; Caliban found himself there as a humble friend whose heart could only conceive one idea, a dog-like gratitude and touching fidelity, obedience without a murmur and passive meekness.

What did they lack? The chemist adored his wife, the wife adored her husband; their hearts were only one, and all their nights were illuminated by the "honey moon." How many women would trade their houses, diamonds, adornments, etc., for the simple clothing of the chemist's wife, the cottage and "the rest," as La Fontaine puts it.

The chemist, happy with his experiment, had therefore decreed that his dear Abel would be nourished in such principles; that his heart would be left to develop, as well as his fine body, as indulgent nature pleased; that he would not be tormented by trying to teach him dismal sciences too soon. His mother, his tender mother, who looked at him fondly, his father, who loved him, Caliban and the dog became his entire universe, the cottage his temple of innocence, the garden his greatest space; and when he was playing, six pebbles and the mud kept him amused or a long time. Thus, the chemist kept him in a reasoned, and perhaps reasonable, obscurantism.

His happy child never complained; the naïve laughter of ignorant infancy was his language, his slightest gesture a caress, his speech a sequence of curious interrogations, to which the chemist always responded in such a manner as to further the system that he had adopted for his dear Abel's future life. He flattered himself all the more with regard to its success because his science gave him the hope of a long old age; he would have the time to render his son as philosophical as himself.

The mother, certain that her husband was a living image of God, believed that he was acting for the best and conformed to his designs; in any case there was not a great enough force of mind within her to perceive objections. She would, as we have seen, have made an excellent government minister, thinking of nothing but her son, finding everything good, and believing what was said to her as an article of faith. As a wife, she was right, for she felt a tranquil and pure happiness invade her through all her pores, and, owing that happiness to her husband, she said to herself: *My son will be as happy as him, and like me*.

However, the good chemist, prescient and wise, calculated everything, for he informed his wife that he had buried under the hearth of the great fireplace in his laboratory a talisman against all the difficulties that she and his son might encounter if he were to die as a result of some accident—but he warned her that she should only raise the stone when she and her son left the cottage in order to go to live somewhere else. Then, having gathered all his books together in one place, arranged his test tubes, his instruments his bottles and his retorts, he did not devote himself to chemistry as much as before. He made a little treasure to subsidize the expenses the Abel might cause, and set up a bed at the back of the laboratory in order to have the dear child always before his eyes.

All that only happened gradually; Abel, in the midst of joy and a veritable child of nature, grew up and soon reached the age of fifteen. The chemist was then fifty and the mother forty. The father with white hair—for study and application produce that effect of aging—devoted all his time to guiding Abel in his preferred route, and only devoted himself to chemistry occasionally, in order not to lose what he had acquired The tradition regarding the devil's cottage still endured, and no event troubled the happiness of the charming family.

Chapter III
The Worthy Chemist Dies

The lapse of time that went by between the tableau presented in the first chapter and the epoch with which we are about to occupy ourselves had brought about changes that require a further description.

They no longer went to bed with the sun. In winter, at five o'clock, Caliban lit a lamp filled with an oil fabricated by the chemist. The latter sat on the worm-eaten armchair, his wife took the stool, Caliban cleaned his grains at one end of the table and the door was closed. The old man with white hair, the jaundiced complexion and the visage full of wrinkles that the lamplight rendered even more obvious, held the *Cabinet des fées*, and, seduced by the supplications of a handsome young man, had consented to teach him to read the tales of enchantment whose illustrations had been the charm of his childhood. The mother listened to her son spell them out as if his difficult, repeated and fastidious tones were the music of the heavenly angels.

For her part, she had learned to embroider, and to decorate the turned-down collar of her son's shirt with a festoon that the father had drawn in blue ink, or sowed a Medieval garment that she had succeeded in copying from an illustration of Prince Charming. Now, as people in Paris at that time were wearing short frock-coats and trousers ceased in the middle and at the bottom like those of Turks, that garment was not at all ridiculous, and rendered her son a thousand times more handsome than Percinet, the lover of Gracieuse.

Indeed, between the chemist's wife and her husband, a young man of sixteen was standing respectfully. He was a good enough height, admirably well-proportioned, with a distinguished stance and an uncommon elegance. His fiery eyes radiated candor and innocence, his brow, as pure as Diana's and as pale as ivory, brought out the jet-black of his hair, which fell in waves over his snow-white shoulders. His face had the flower of youth, the vivacity of color and elasticity of the features, the virginal appearance and gracious pride, which realize in our eyes the idea we have of young Greeks or angels. His almond-shaped eyes with long lashes only quit the book over which his rosy fingers were wandering to obtain a soft glance from his mother, and often, when he had read an entire sentence, he deposited on the serene forehead of the old man one of the kisses that a young adolescent, still ignorant, imprints with the torment of a secret fire.

Caliban often stopped work to admire surreptitiously, as a masterpiece of nature, the idol of his mother; and it seemed that everything was smiling on the virtuous group gathered under the black vault, in the midst of the furnaces and the chemical apparatus, like a bouquet of wild flowers blooming in a lair cluttered with rubble.

In his childhood, Abel had derived his sweetest joy from looking at the illustrations of tales of enchantment; at sixteen, he was trying to read them; those magical adventures were the subject of all his meditations, and the force of his reason in all the sap of its first development, was directed toward the charm of enchantments. His ignorance and naivety contributed to make him believe in the charming creatures known as fays, for he never conceived the thought of casting doubt on the veracity of storytellers; then again, that cheerful mythology of modernity was so much in rapport with his tender soul, disposed to the mild religion of mystery, that it would have hurt him to be disillusioned. He was so convinced of the reality of tales of enchantment and the brilliant inventions of the Orient that he never even asked any questions of his father.

Thus, for two or three years, helping his father in his chemical endeavors, helping Caliban to look after the garden, walking in the forest with his father, and in the evening, reading to his family the dreams of the Thousand-and-One Nights, etc., made up an existence of joy and happiness for him. His naivety and generosity, the excellence of his good qualities, blossomed, and the good chemist applauded himself, along with his wife, in anticipating that their son, their happiness and joy, would be as delighted as they were in that modest habitation, with a pretty wife by his side and some other Caliban.

But heaven had decided that it would be otherwise.

In fact, one day, when the chemist was working at his furnaces, his son and his wife left him alone and closed the laboratory door. The old man, who was on the point of discovering the secret of making gold, had spent several sleepless nights; he fell asleep with fatigue, and the deleterious vapors of the charcoal stifled him.

On returning from their walk in the forest, the chemist's wife and Abel found Caliban weeping, on his knees before his master. The wife was rooted to the spot; Abel tried to lift his father up, but found him cold; then he held the old man's head on his knees and tried to bring him back to life by the force of kisses. In the end, he understood the idea of death, and covered his expired father with tears. The chemist had on his face the mildness that had made the charm of his life and that of those around him. The scene, eloquent with dolor, resembled the one in which Raphael represents Christ brought down from the cross, between his mother, an apostle and an angel.

At night, covered by the mantle of soft light that the moon casts upon such dolorous scenes, the three inhabitants of the cottage laid the body of their friend in a ditch that Caliban dug while weeping. The wind was agitating the foliage, and the queen of the night, sending one of her purest rays, seemed to be participating in the death of the just man; the dawn found the group kneeing before the mound of earth. No one had yet pronounced a word, and the silence was only troubled by the concert of birds.

"They're announcing to us," Abel said, then, "that my father's soul has risen to the heavens...but it has passed through the flowers with which his grave is covered."

"Do you believe that?" the mother replied, looking alternately at Abel and the grave.

"Certainly," said Abel.

"Oh, let me think," the chemist's wife went on, "that it is all as you say!" And, a sweet hope slipping into her desolate heart, she leaned her head on her son's bosom, as if to drown her chagrin there.

Caliban, without hearing anything, never ceased gazing at his adored master's grave; and, far from regretting that all the sciences were buried there with him, he only saw one thing: his master; which is to say, his whole existence. The mute expression of that profound dolor was well worth that of a city maidservant who, when her mistress dies, on receiving one of her dresses, asks whether there are any remnants of the fabric.

The three inhabitants of the cottage went silently back into the laboratory, all of whose furniture still reminded them of the beloved chemist. They found a little sweetness in those memories, but for a long time their interior offered them the image of the grief painted in *The Return of Sextus*.[4] The mother and son often remained idle, gazing at the furnace, and Caliban wept when he lit the lamp, because the oil that the chemist had made would eventually run out, and he thought that he could not make any more of it for them.

It was not until some time after that painful epoch that Abel engraved on the chemist's grave words that the Oriental jinni living in his head doubtless dictated to him:

As the young woman on the banks of the Ganges consults the future of her amours by putting a light boat made of palm-leaves on the river, and follows with her eyes the light that she has placed therein, we have laden a frail hull with all our hope and happiness; our light shines therein; the shipwreck is complete.

A year later, Abel had to change his epitaph slightly, because the chemist's wife did not have enough, in the love of her son, to keep her alive, and she was buried beside the man whose faithful companion she had been.

Abel, who was inconsolable, did not leave the cottage; he no longer opened the *Cabinet des Fées* and knew no universe but the laboratory where he had played with his beloved father and mother. At dusk he went outside and went slowly to sit down beneath a weeping willow beside his parents' graves.

---

[4] Although it is not the only representation of the subject, the reference is certainly to *The Return of Marcus Sextus* by Pierre-Narcisse, Baron Guérin, first exhibited at the Paris Salon in 1799, where it was met with great acclaim, inspiring numerous literary tributes.

Caliban did not say a word, but ardently respired the sweet emanations of flowers that the breeze rocked gently over the two graves, believing that he was breathing in his masters' souls. The evening star often surprised them in the middle of a somber reverie.

Abel, the child of nature, pleased himself in his grief, without seeking to shake it off like a city-dweller, and sometimes, when his excessively oppressed heart could not contain the host of pure and virgin thoughts of his chaste soul, he spoke to Caliban with the poetic energy of the savage.

"Listen," he said. "The light of that star is not as brilliant as the brightness spread over our lives by their sweet presence. We lived through them; why have we not died, since they are no longer?

"This garden is a desert; its flowers no longer please me; the moon, which smiled at me once, hides in the clouds without my regretting her light; and I only like the harmonious sound of the wind in the forest, because it sometimes brings me the debris of their voices, speaking to me from the height of heaven.

"Let us cultivate these roses; they are born among their ashes, and their odor is their soul; this lily is my mother and that lilac with odorous clusters is my father, whose knowledge is resolved in perfumes..."

Caliban understood that song of dolor, and if some bird sang he chased it away gently, for its joy was importunate to them. It was thus that those two innocent souls were always confounded in the same dream, and the same regrets. They were Christians without knowing it.

One evening, Caliban said to Abel: "Abel, the storm curbs the flower, but it gets up again..."

"There are some that it breaks," the young man replied.

Caliban was unable to reply, but he wept—was that not a response?

Those two beings remained devoid of ideas, knowledge and help for a long time, in the midst of society, as if on a desert island surrounded by the Ocean.

After a few months, however, Abel began to read tales of enchantment again in the evening—but soon he only read them in the morning, because Caliban observed to him that they were using up the oil fabricated by his father, and that it was necessary to conserve it in order that it might last them for as long as they lived.

Caliban listened to the tales, and they soothed one another by sharing their thoughts about the nature of fays. Eventually, Abel ended up desiring to see a fay, but he did not know what to do in order to evoke one. He read and reread, and saw that fays always came of their own accord when someone was unhappy. Then he said to Caliban: "Why have we not seen fays already…? Oh! I've guessed it…my father was a djinni, my mother a fay…and they've abandoned us! They'll come back!"

That day, he crowned himself with roses, and hope was born in his heart; he became cheerful again, as in the days when he played on his mother's bosom, when he had called her the Good Fay, and the desire often took him to lift the stone in the fireplace; but, remembering that his mother had told him that it was necessary for him to be unhappy and ready to go live somewhere else, he could not resolve to leave his father's cottage. He even paid scrupulous attention to not disturbing anything in the laboratory, which remained in the same state in which the chemist had left it. The cult of children of nature for objects of their veneration is full of the most gracious attentions, and their mourning is nobler than that depicted by garments; the mourning of the soul is the religion of pain; that of the body is a devotion.

"I'm sure," Abel said to Caliban, gazing at the fireplace with a keen curiosity, that there is an entrance to a subterranean palace under there, like the garden from which Aladdin obtained his lamp; that the steps are made of sapphire, the columns of diamond, the fruits of gold, the pomegranates filed with ruby pips; that in shaking the roses there would be showers of gold and silver; that a little fay with her magic wand is sitting on a throne of mother-of-pearl there, and that she is as beautiful as a morning in spring; there are hummingbirds there, and she has a chariot harnessed to doves, and she would enable me to see my father and mother again."

"But Abel," said Caliban, "you talk like a book..."

It was a curious spectacle to see that old and deformed servant beside Abel, whose forms, beauty, soft gaze and disordered hair gave the idea of an angel conversing with a demon.

Often Abel said to Caliban: "You're ugly, Caliban, because you're not the son of a fay, like me. Look how the flower reddens and fades away, how the nightingale dies after having sung, how often a storm flattens our rose-bushes, and how the other day an oak much taller than me was felled...but I don't change, my voice is resounding, my cheeks are colored, my eyes shine, and I remain handsome, because I'm the son of a fay."

"That's true," said Caliban. "I'm from Le Mans."

"What is Le Mans?" asked Abel.

"It's a place where there are a lot of people and authorities; it's a city."

"A city like those in our tales, with princes, mandarins and princesses?"

"And fattened pullets," added Caliban—but when he tried to explain what a fattened pullet was,[5] he could not do it; it seemed that he would never be able to explain what influence a fattened pullet might exert on the conduct of a man."

That was the state in which Abel found himself at the age of eighteen; the sum of all his ideas was in the *Cabinet des fées*; his life was all contemplative and dream-filed, an ideal, and the force of his rich imagination and his Oriental soul went toward chimerical beings; he spoke in a language full of images and Oriental comparisons, and his intelligence was open to all superstitions.

Meanwhile, the village that he often saw, without wanting to go there, since his father had forbidden him to do so—and he did not want to mingle with people anyway—had been subject to great changes with regard to the ideas that had once been conceived regarding the devil's cottage. To begin with, when people learned of the death of the chemist and that of his wife, they began to lose a little of the terror that he cottage on the hill inspired; secondly, smoke was no longer seen coming out of the terrible chimney; and that change produced the greatest effect. Finally, the young people who had once been taken away to fight came back, with diplomas, and treated as "conscripts" those who said that the devil had lived in the neighborhood.

Then people became ashamed of believing that they had been any danger in going to the chemist's cottage, and Jacques Bontems, a sergeant in the cuirassiers of the

---

[5] I have translated Caliban's *poularde* [fattened pullet] literally, but it is more than likely that he intends its metaphorical meaning, which is to a loose woman or prostitute.

guard, proved to them that the beadle was nothing but a fool but that his daughter had no peer in the world, and that, when one had "been at the tit" in Moscow, Spain and in Egypt, where there was "a damnable sun that dried out your noggin," one knew all about the devil and girls...

It is only in that epoch that the story we are telling really begins, and what has preceded it belongs to the category of things that the spectator needs to know before the curtain goes up—but now, the curtain is going up.

Chapter IV
What a Fay Often Is

The last part of the preceding chapter introduced Jacques Bontems and Catherine, the beadle's daughter.

Now, you need to know that Grandvani, the beadle, was an important person. After being beadle he had become Maire, and the richest man in the village, because he had had the good sense to buy the property of the Church during the Revolution, in order, he said, that it should not pass out of the hands of the clergy. As he was a part of the clergy, he believed that the fire of heaven would not descend upon him, and he had acquired the property "because he had good intentions." Privately, however, he promised himself to enjoy it to the full.

One can, therefore, imagine how, twenty years later, he could be very well off, having bought a great deal for very little. His daughter Catherine was the prettiest young woman in the village, as he was the richest man, and she found herself the objective of the desires of a host of suitors. The girls in Paris did not always have as many.

Jacques Bontems, whose acquaintance we have just made via the specimen of his language reported, perhaps too faithfully, in the preceding chapter, was a former cuirassier, dismissed without a pension because he only had twenty years of service, and he was eating through what remained of his army pay in order to put on a good show and marry Catherine. He had written to one of his former comrades, who was a clerk in the Ministry of Finance, in order that he could put a word in and obtain the position of the commune's tax-collector for him, claiming that the man holding the position was a *"perruque"* who had *"straw in his clogs"*—an expression extracted literally from his letter. He hoped to marry Catherine if he succeeded in getting the old tax-collector sacked, and left no stone unturned to arrive at his goal.

The sergeant was the best fellow in the world; he had won a medal at Austerlitz, but, having returned to his homeland, he wanted to support his red ribbon with his discourse, and attributed a credit to himself that he did not have. Let us say that Jacques Bontems was something of a braggart, but let us also say for his justification that he had been driven to it to some extent by the desire to exalt the glory of France and the ascendancy of brave men like him over other men, but most of all to make the Maire believe that in him he would have a powerful son-in-law; if you add to that a natural disposition to exaggeration, you will readily pardon him.

Thus, he had no scruple about diminishing the number of our regiments at Bautzen and doubling the number of enemies; in saying that he had entered Stettin with fifteen cavaliers and General Lasalle, and that the sixteen had taken the city with thirty-two saber-cuts and a gallop. The peasants, in a circle, pricked up their ears and opened their eyes as wide as the coaching entrance of a Duc's town house, when the sergeant told them that a clever little drummer-boy armed with his two sticks often made a tour of enemy advance posts and brought back fifty Cossacks with their horses, tack, lances, sheepskins and all.

After he had said that it was ordinary to leap through the embrasure of a cannon, while it was being hauled back after having spat out its grapeshot, and take possession, as one of five, of a battery that was hindering the "little shaver" in his operations, he turned up the tips of his moustache, tapped the ash out of his pipe, shook his head and said: "That's how one wins a medal!" Then, if one of his comrades made the observation in a corner that that was an act of courage that one only attempted with the devil in one's body, Bontems, darting a masterly wink at him, replied: "Leave it out, old man! It's necessary to maintain national morale!" The other, before such a grave consideration, maintained silence, and on his own behalf, outbid Monsieur Bontems.

Thus, the sergeant, a man of five feet six inches, with a sun-tanned face and a martial stride, and the free and easy manners of our cosmopolitan cuirassiers, had succeeded in persuading the beadle that he knew great generals, Councilors of State, and even the Court, and that he had credit there.

For a long time, a legal dispute had been going on between a neighboring commune and the one the Maire administered, over the wealth of the two communes that remained undivided. Each commune wanted to have more than the other, and for ten years had been going to court, obtaining decrees and edicts, and the affair was not over. The Maires did not have the means to go to Paris, to follow advocates, judges and ministers, and to spend enormous amounts on dinners, carriages and presents, and the communes even less, so the Maire, not refusing to believe Bontems' discourse, asked him, as proof of his credit, to sort out an affair in which he was involved and which had only thus far got to the Council of the Prefecture.

Jacques, as a prudent man, had begun by asking for time and was determined, in the interim, to makes such headway with Mademoiselle Catherine that she would fall in love with him. After that, he promised himself to handle the matter so well that the Maire could not do otherwise that marry him to Catherine—or, rather, propose to him that he marry Catherine.

He passed off his correspondence with an office clerk as a correspondence with the chiefs, and as his comrade addressed letters to him in with the ministry's seal, Jacques Bontems gave the appearance of a man of importance when the envelopes that he as careful to leave lying around were found. If he were able to obtain the position of tax-collector he would have crowned his enterprise with a complete success, and the entire region would be prostrate before his power. Would anyone even know whether he had paid the contributions, if, after such a fine exploit, he had been nominated as a député by the surrounding communes? Then, more than one of the expressions that was said to escape from representatives during the storm of important sessions would be heard on the legislative benches.

The village was, as can be seen, prey to intrigues as difficult and numerous as those of the *Marriage of Figaro*. The tax-collector was the target of darts hurled by Bontems, who wanted his place, and he defended himself courageously; hence, parties for and against, speeches, hints, opinions and disputes. Jacques Bontems, however, put on a polite face toward the tax-collector, and the tax-collector toward Bontems; it was just as at Court: nothing was lacking except gilded clothing, fine language, carriages and the sound of ministries collapsing.

Abel and Caliban floated over all these intrigues like the sage that Lucretius represents contemplating from the height of the clouds the earth and its inhabitants, incessantly running after gold and fortune.

The fortunate Abel lived in the magical world of goblins, sprites, djinni, fays, enchanters, princes, lovely princesses and enchanted gardens compared with which the terrestrial paradise was devoid of charm. He was waiting for a fay as the Jews wait the Messiah; he read and reread the tales, and after having read them he told Caliban that he experienced the desire to fly into the sky, to seize a gilded cloud and go to listen on the summit of a rock for the ethereal sounds that would betray the abode of the brilliant angels.

He had imagined a fay, and adored her; when, one evening, a shooting star lit up and a long furrow of light shone in the air, he ran into the forest, to the tree where he fiery cloud had stopped, and he was desolate to have missed the fay.

If, by night, a harmonious breeze slid through the foliage and caressed the garden, he shouted: "Caliban, my fay is passing by!" They waited; Caliban raised his nose, remaining bewildered, and poor Abel, after having searched or a long time, returned sadly. The following morning, if he perceived fresh flowers opening, he said that the fay had looked at his garden.

Finally, he saw fays during his sleep; and, waking up with a start, he listened, gathering all of his force of audition, and mistook the soft murmur of the wind for the debris of the provocative and mocking laughter of an impertinent fay.

One morning, he was sitting at the door of the cottage on the stone that served him as a bench; he was clad in a frock-coat of sorts and his Turkish trousers; His beautiful embroidered shirt, open at the top, permitted the sight of his lovely neck, and his hair, as curly as that of Antinous, gave him the appearance of a god of antiquity reading Homer to see whether the poet had depicted him accurately. The vine seemed to take pleasure in shading the chemist's son with its branch; the dew was shining in the grass where his feet rested; there were flowers around him, and he wore them on his head.

He was there, reading the story of the two children of the fay who wore stars on their foreheads, when he suddenly heard at a distance the light footsteps of a woman whose dress seemed to be quivering. His imagination working, he waited with a sort of anxiety for the person who was still hidden by a bush.

He soon saw a young woman advancing toward him, simply dressed, her black hair escaping beneath a headscarf elegantly knotted about her head. Her stride was light and brisk. She had a red corsage and a white dress, and her face was shining with a dazzling freshness. She was pale; the roundness of her bare arms seemed polished, and her charming hands would have done honor to more than one beautiful lady. Her face expressed naivety, and a pure grace, without affectation, decorated her movements.

She was coming up the path quite rapidly, but as soon as she saw Abel she stopped, contemplated him with a surprise mingled with admiration, and her gaze seemed to blush. She did not notice immediately the avidity that Abel deployed in the attention with which he was examining her, but she soon lowered her eyes, and appeared to deliberate within herself as to whether she would or would not go past the cottage.

In the same way that there are certain men who, in their poses, their gait and the ensemble of their being, contain dignity and strength, there are women who combine to a high degree of perfection *that which is woman*, and who are surrounded by a cortege of seduction, attractions, graces and pretty mannerisms. The young woman had much more of that than was necessary to turn the head of a young man who had only ever seen Caliban, his mother and an old chemist at his furnace.

After a moment of silence and examination, Abel launched himself forward rapidly; the young woman retreated, but the great beauty of the young man, and, above all, the candor that radiated from his entire person, ensured that she only fled as far as the bush. Abel followed her there and, taking her by her hand, which he felt trembling, he said to her in the enchanting tone of the most touching voice that one could ever hear:

"You're not a fay, because your hand is trembling; you're blushing, you're walking on the ground and you have no wand; but you're as pretty as a fay..."

The young woman withdrew her hand, and did not understand any of that speech, except that it was flattering. She did not reply, but she looked at Abel in a fashion to make him understand that she would not forget a single word of what he had just said, and that she would search for its meaning for a long time.

"Come and sit down beside me on my stone," he said to her, accompanying his words with an inviting smile.

They went there; for a moment, silence still reigned, and it was Abel who broke it, saying: "I'd like to sit beside you often."

The young woman replied: "You do me honor..."

Abel looked at her anxiously, as if to ask her what she meant by those words, but she continued, saying: "It's you who live in this cottage?"

"Yes," he replied. "And you, you come from the village over there? I can't go there, because my father and mother forbade me to; that makes me sorry now."

"Ah! You can't come?" she said, with a naïve tone of regret.

"No," Abel replied, "But you can come to my cottage; it's very beautiful. You'll see the clothes of which father the enchanter made use when he lived on this earth; I conserve them carefully, with those of my mother the fay."

The young woman looked at him with a profound astonishment, and the more she looked at him, the more she admired the rare beauty of that gentle marvel of amour.

"You doubtless have a name," he continued, ingenuously, "like all princesses. Without knowing yours, I would name you Charme-du-Coeur."

"Oh!" she said. "My name is Catherine..."

"What does that mean?" he asked, thinking that her name signified some quality, like the names of princesses in Arabic tales.

"It signifies that I'm the daughter of Monsieur Grandvani, the Maire of the village."

At that moment, Caliban, who was in the cottage, hearing another voice than that if his young master, came out—but when he showed his hideous head the young woman was afraid, and fled.

Abel watched her go, and stood up in order to follow her with his eyes. When Caliban asked him who she was, he told him: "It's a young woman almost as beautiful as Gracieuse. How can I see her again? Perhaps she's a fay in disguise..."

As she fled, Catherine thought about the young man, and when she arrived in the village she had already reasoned sufficiently to promise herself to hide the encounter she had just had from everyone. The more she thought about it, the less she could convince herself that Abel was a human being; he seemed to her so dissimilar to the people she saw every day that she was include to

48

think he had a superior nature. She never stopped thinking about that celestial face, the brilliant coloring, the freshness and naivety of Abel; that evening Jacques Bontems perceived that she was responding obliquely to his questions, and that she was distracted.

For his part, Abel thought a great deal about the being, new to him, that he had seen that morning in reality. The tales of enchantment that he meditated had informed him about human sentiments; he was not unaware that "amour" existed, because every tale was based, like all the tales in the world, on two persecuted lovers. But the works he read never told him enough about that matter, and all that he could conclude was the axiom that a man loves a woman and reciprocally, that a woman loves a man. For himself, he could only love a fay, and the impression that the lovely Catherine had produced in him was far from attaining the perfection that a fay would have made him experience. The more he contemplated himself, however, the more he found that Catherine's image was engraved in his heart.

The next day, and the days thereafter, he ran in the morning to place himself on the path, returning to sit on the stone and wait for Catherine. On the fourth day, he saw her coming in the distance; she was walking slowly, while looking around.

He went to met her and, bringing her back silently to his rustic bench, he contemplated her for a moment and then said: "Catherine—for I've remembered your name—you're more ornamented than the other day. You have a rose in your hair; your bosom is covered with a dewy fabric and your hands are embellished by a circle of gold..." He stopped, and looked at her, as if waiting for her reply.

Catherine blushed more deeply and lowered her eyes; but, thinking about the ignorance of the young unknown, she raised them again and said: "In the world where I come from, we often change adornment for the people we wish to please."

"Can one please someone by means one's clothes?" he replied, with vivacity. "Oh, how I'd like to have fine ones, if ever I encounter a fay!"

"What is a fay?" asked Catherine.

"A fay," Abel replied, smiling "is a divine spirit that puts on human form and appears to us carried on a cloud. Fays are dressed in robes that resemble the azure of the skies; their face is as soft and scintillating as a star; they walk over flowers without trampling them and nourish themselves on nectar, like bees. They drink the dew, and live in the cups of flowers. Often, a fay glides along a branch and descends like a light and brilliant flame; she embellishes nature, reigns there as a sovereign, makes all those she protects happy, and gives them talismans against misfortune. Often, she even takes them to palaces with columns of gold and diamond, the paving stones of which are marble and the vaults like those of the sky. In sum, she surrounds you with a host of magic spells and happiness…and that enchantment falls on you from the sky, one morning or one night, unexpectedly."

"In that case," said Catherine, "amour is a fay that one has in one's heart." And her eyes, resplendent with tenderness, came to be confounded with Abel's in a gaze of admiration.

"Amour," said Abel, taking Catherine's hand, "is a word that isn't new to me, but I can't conceive all that it expresses."

At that ingenuous remark, Catherine felt her heart swell. She withdrew her hand gently and put it to her eyes in order to wipe away the shiny tears that were forming there.

Tender and naïve, Abel drew closer to her without saying a word, and tried to collect Catherine's tears with his long, dark, wavy hair.

"Amour," the pretty peasant girl said then, "is a suffering..."

"Oh, no!" Abel continued. "One ought to be happy. If my fay presents herself to my gaze, I sense that I shall love her; then I wouldn't dare approach her; I would respect her and admire her without saying anything to her, for it would seem to me that speaking might soil her soul; I would be content to think about her. I wouldn't take her by the hand as with you, but I would love to respire the flower whose perfume she had respired; and if it were a rose, it would then have an odor a thousand times sweeter. I would prefer to feel pain with her than pleasure with others; when she had gone, I would still see her, always. She would be my mother, my father and my sister all at the same time: everything to me. Everything would come to me from her: light, happiness, joy. If she spoke far away from me, I would sense her words, for I would accompany her everywhere. In sum, I would live in her, she would be my morning, my day, my sun, more than all nature..."

"Enough! Enough!" said Catherine, sobbing.

"You're weeping?" he said. "Why? Are you in pain?"

"Yes," she said. "Look, that village you can see is nothing but pains and torments." And Catherine, deflecting his attention, described for him the intrigues and troubles of the hamlet.

Abel did not understand any of that speech, except that the people it concerned were unhappy. Then he exclaimed: "Well then, let them do as I do! Let them have a cottage, a garden, and they'll be happy. Let them come here—I'll console them!"

"There are misfortunes that can't be soothed..."

"That's true," said Abel, thinking about his grief when he had lost his father. "But they haven't all seen their parents die?"

"Oh," she said, "there are other woes. We have in the valley a young woman whose story I'll tell you, the next time I come...if I come...and you tell me if she can be consoled..."

"If you come?" repeated Abel. "Why wouldn't you come?"

Catherine tried to make him understand the ideas of propriety and morality that are the basis of society, but Abel did not understand any of it, and replied: "I don't know why you're forbidden down there to do what gives you pleasure."

Catherine looked at Abel for a long time with a painful sentiment, and went away slowly.

Chapter V
Amour in the Village

Catherine, a young woman devoid of education, ignorant and naïve, nevertheless perceived Abel's ingenuousness, and could not explain it. What he had said to her about fays was for her the object of great mediations. Finally, she consulted the curé in order to discover whether fays existed.

The curé, a sufficiently learned man, easily deduced, from the nature of Catherine's questions, that she had a powerful motive for asking them; then, it was quite natural that he should confess the young woman. Catherine, too simple to resist the curé's questions, told him everything that had happened.

The latter fell into a profound astonishment on learning that a young man so close to the state of nature existed in the present century. Ignorant of the circumstances that had brought Abel to that point of credulity and savagery, the curé imagined that he was a young man who had lost his mind, and he strove to demonstrate to Catherine that she was running grave dangers in the company of that extraordinary being. He also proved to her that fays were imaginary individuals created by pure fantasy, and to make her understand he read her and explained to her the tale of Peau-d'âne, a fable by La Fontaine, and an Oriental tale, and he urged her not to return to the hill again.

Catherine, on leaving the curé, thought that Abel was not mad, and that she was not running any danger in his company except the greatest danger of all: that of loving without the hope of being loved. In order to succeed, she resolved to make one last effort with her friend on the mountain, by telling him the story of the young female reaper.

She therefore went one morning, and, casually sitting down beside him, she began by telling him that fays did not exist; then she tried to make him understand the curé's arguments.

"Catherine," Abel replied, gravely, "no one will ever prove to me that there is only us in nature. Who is it that has made all that we see? It's a great djinni. There is the fay of the flowers, the fay of the waters, the fay of the air. Are you not borne, like me to love something outside yourself?"

"Oh yes," she said.

"Well, can you not imagine flowers that don't fade, and a day that has no night? All of that is found in the land of the fays; the fays live beyond the skies, for the skies are the parvis of their temple and the stars are their footprints. When a tempest covers the sky it's because the evil djinn have escaped from their prisons or have broken the bottles in which they were enclosed. Catherine, don't you sometimes have a desire to be elsewhere than where you are? Don't you desire to fly in the air, and confound yourself in an amorous adoration like that I have for a fay?"

"Yes," she said, very softly, "I'm a Christian and I love God."

"God!" said Abel. "Who is he?"

"It's him who made us in his image, to serve and adore him," she said, in accordance with her catechisms.

"Oh, I understand," said Abel. "God is the king of fays and djinn."

"But the curé told me that there were no fays," she said, with chagrin.

"Who is the curé?" asked Abel, immediately.

It was impossible for Catherine to make Abel understand what a curé was. She embarked on an explanation of the social order, but could not finish her explanation because she became entangled within it. Finally, she gave up, concluding that a curé was a man who did not marry because he had to love no one other than God, to pray to him for everyone, and to dress in black.

"One doesn't pray to God oneself, then?" Abel said, and went on: "But if your curé has shown you in a book that fays don't exit, I can show you in another that they do!" He ran to fetch a volume of tales, and showed her the illustration of the apparition of the fay Abricotine.

"Since you want there to be fays, I'll believe in them," she said, blushing, "And if even if there aren't, believe that your error is sweeter to me than the truth."

"Catherine," he said, with the infantile joy and naïve curiosity of a young squirrel running from branch to branch, playing with every fruit, "you promised me a story; will you tell it to me, for I love to hear you speak…?"

Catherine then felt a movement in her heart that strongly resembled that of fear.

In fact, her own fate was about to be decided.

The Story of the Young Reaper

"At the last harvest," she said, indicating the fields of the valley, "there came from Lorraine—that's a distant country where the inhabitants are poor and come in spring to help with our crops—there came, as I said, a young woman, with her mother. They were both very poor. The mother was old, but in spite of her infirmities, she made the journey with her daughter.

"Her daughter's name is Juliette; she's as pretty as a rose that is just opened, and under her big straw hat, with her blonde hair, she's like a violet hiding under a dry leaf. Her arms are round and as smooth as the branch of a young birch tree, and once, her smile was as gracious as a spring morning. They both came to that farm you can see in the distance, on the far side of the village; they asked to help with the harvest, and it was permitted to them.

"The farmer has a son, a handsome young man, tall, well-made and sun-tanned; he does the plowing and drives the carts; he's the most skillful in the village at shooting with a bow; he knows how to read and write, and sings in the church on Sunday. Finally, it's him who directs the harvesters and all the farm workers.

"He was in the farmhouse when Juliette and her mother presented themselves; as soon Juliette saw him, she went pale and felt disposed to love him, because he was handsome."

"If I loved," said Abel, interrupting, "I'd only love for beauty..."

"Juliette apparently supposed," Catherine went on, "that the young man's soul was like the envelope, and the poor child, before knowing whether she would be paid in return, let herself cherish the farmer's son.

"Then, she only ever reaped in the fields where he was; she watched him covertly, and if he stopped somewhere, she could not bear anyone else to cut the ears that he had brushed. If he sat down on a sheaf, she put its stalks on her head. In sum, she always tried to be near him, so that, when he complained about the heat, she presented him with an earthenware jug full of water, which she carried with her, and which became sacred to her as soon as his lips had touched it; it was noticed that she could no longer bear her poor mother to drink from it. And she preferred, poor as she was, to buy another, and, in spite of her weakness, to carry two instead of one.

"When Antoine spoke, she trembled inside, and collected the slightest sounds of that cherished voice; if he spoke to her, she blushed and dared not look at him. In sum, she loved him with all the force of her soul, seizing the present moment ardently and not thinking about the future.

"The mother perceived that her daughter had changed, for, while still having as much love for her, Juliette had distractions. One day, when Antoine had helped Juliette to pick up her bundle, and their hands and gazes had met, she let her mother carry the burden of which she was accustomed to relieve her.

"Then, that evening, the mother said to Juliette: 'My child, the air of this region doesn't suit you; let's go back to Lorraine,' Juliette replied that, for her, Lorraine was now here. The mother saw that there was no longer any remedy, and they continued bringing in the crop.

"Antoine was not unaware for long of the amorous feelings that Juliette had for him, because he saw her one night, in the farmyard, sitting on a stone and not sleeping; she was looking by turns at the sky and the part of the house where he slept. As it was dark and she thought everyone was asleep, that everything was quiet, and nothing could be heard but he sound of the clouds rolling through the air, she blew a kiss toward Antoine's bedroom. That mute and silent adoration, that secret amour, pleased the young man, who became more attentive to Juliette thereafter than he had been before...

"Are you listening?" Catherine asked Abel.

"Yes, yes," replied the young man, who seemed to be dreaming.

Then Catherine repeated her phrase, looking at him, and continued: "And Antoine gave Juliette less work than the others. When it was too hot he told her to rest, and she rested with her mother, because it was him that had said it to them. At table, he made sure that she was well served, and one day, he put a flower in her place. Juliette took the flower, and hid it in her bosom—and that flower, although withered, is still there.

"One evening, when everyone was in bed, Juliette and Antoine went to sit down under a tree in the garden of the farm and they talked for a long time. Antoine was charmed by the young woman's grace and wit. From then on they loved one another ardently, and in secret. Juliette was very happy when she saw that her love was shared by the man she adored, and she yielded enthusiastically to the hope that nothing could oppose their happiness.

"When she saw that Antoine was smitten with her, they exchanges roles; it was Antoine who amorously embraced everything she carried or touched; he watched her reaping, and helped her, as well as her mother, who, in spite of her long experience, began to believe that it would all end well. Then the old mother smiled, on seeing the farmer's son dance with Juliette in the evenings, and not embracing her in the quadrille, where everyone embraces, which seemed to her to be a good augury.

"Finally, one evening, coming back to the farm, Juliette who had taken Antoine's arm, said to him: 'My friend, whom I love amorously, you've given me a flower of the earth and a thousand other flowers that come from the heavens; in return, I can give you this ribbon that serves me as a belt; take it, and remember that, in offering it to you, I'm giving you myself.'

"Antoine took the ribbon, and kept it; he wanted a kiss, but Juliette refused.

"They came to understand one another with a glance, to read in their eyes, and could no longer be apart. They confounded their hearts and savored the delights of a delicate and pure love. For them, there was no more time or weather, no season or earth; they were all soul, and individuality had ceased; for they finished up adopting one another's gestures, speech and mannerisms, thinking alike; in sum, Antoine was all Juliette, and Juliette all Antoine.

"Then, one morning, when Juliette had been weeping because the farmer had talked about the end of the harvest and paying the reapers, Antoine told his father that he loved Juliette and wanted to marry her. That same evening, the farmer, who wanted to marry his son to me, threw Juliette off his farm, after giving her what he owed her; then he told his son that he would never consent to his marriage with the young woman from Lorraine, because she was too poor.

"Juliette left without weeping, but she was as pale as a corpse; she was taken in by another farmer, for whom she and her mother work without being paid, but she doesn't want to leave the area where Antoine lives, and the poor girl is still glad to breathe the air that he breathes.

"I went to find her one morning and I said to her: 'Juliette, be certain that I will never marry Antoine, and if you need anything, you've found a friend in me who will help you in anything, with pleasure."

"That's good!" exclaimed Abel, clapping his hands like an overexcited spectator. Catherine was nonplussed, so violent and sweet to her heart was the joy that praise caused her, which only concerned the soul.

"Since that time," she continued, "Juliette has no other pleasure than seeing Antoine in church, and sometimes perceiving him in the fields; they rarely meet, but then they talk to one another with an extreme voluptuousness, swearing themselves one to the other. However, Juliette reproaches herself for having brought the anger of his father down on Antoine's head, because the farmer has told his son that if he doesn't marry the woman he gives him for a wife he'll disinherit him by selling his property. Juliette is sad, and hopeless; she's consuming herself, and resembles a young flower eaten away by a worm. The whole village likes her and pities her, but she's dying of amour.

"Now," Catherine added, "what remedy can you find for such evils?"

Abel remained silent.

"But suppose," Catherine continued, "that Antoine hadn't loved Juliette, and that Juliette had always adored him. Tell me whether there could exist, for a soul full of love, a greater woe?"

As she pronounced the last words, her voice trembled; she looked at Abel with anxiety, and awaited his response, as a summer flower fatigued by the sun awaits the evening dew.

"It seems to me," Abel replied, in an indifferent manner, "that true love always ends up vanquishing all obstacles; the good fays always triumph..."

Will I triumph? Catherine wondered.

From that day on, Catherine often went to talk to Abel, and the poor child loved the chemist's son with the same ardor with which Juliette loved Antoine.

Meanwhile, the rumor spread within the village that there was a young man in the cottage on the hill as beautiful as the day, ravishing and celestial, and that an infernal demon served him; that he had inherited from the chemist the power to command nature; that he had conversations with fays and goblins, which were understood under the name of spirits; and finally, that he was sometimes seen in the evening talking to a revenant that fluttered like a shade. Those rumors ran around the entire area; what accredited them was that the curé preached a sermon forbidding young women to go to the hill.

Meanwhile, Abel loved Catherine, but as a veritable sister, and he still nurtured his sweet dreams. He was all the more devoured by the desire to see a fay because his dreams often offered him fantastic images, which he seized ardently, and which he sometimes believed, on awakening, that he had really seen.

He made his confidences to Catherine, who held back her tears, but who, as she went away, wept to see herself disdained for imaginary beings, which the curé had told her could never exist. She hoped that her turn would come.

She always came to see Abel in the morning, because it was morning when she had met him for the first time, so her excursions to the hill had not yet been noticed by anyone; in any case, her father, knowing her innocence and the horror that he had inspired in her for the hill, did not conceive any suspicion.

However, when Catherine perceived one day that she had to love Abel without any hope of being loved by him, she began to grow pale.

The change in her face and her behavior did not escape the eye of the cuirassier sergeant Jacques Bontems, who paid court to her every evening. He noticed that for some time, he had not been seen as kindly by Cathe-rine—who, comparing him with Abel, whose manners were natural, elegant and naïve, no longer found Bontems' brusque tone, casual gestures and language in good taste. Nevertheless, he still flattered himself that he might marry her, for he had received a letter that gave him a great deal of hope.

In fact, his friend the office clerk had just been promoted to the important position of the minister's personal assistant. It was then that he wrote a petition to the minister to have the position of tax-collector, and he sent it to his friend to put on His Excellency's desk at the first opportunity. He spent a long time drafting his petition, but finally settled, after a fortnight's reflection, on the curious document that we shall transcribe literally.[6]

Monseigneur

Your Excellency will be surprised to learn that in the commune of V*** there is for a tax-collector an old blockhead who, in the machine of with Your Excellency is the soul, is an ungreased wheel: that being so, Jacques Bontems, sergeant, to whom, in parentheses, a retirement pension has been refused because he lacked one year of service, when he had been expressly licensed; given that Your Excellency was not minister then, one could not make him any reproach, but he is nevertheless without pension.

However, that being by the by, a matter concluded, let's not talk about it anymore: then, he will get to the nub of the matter, and without making a fuss, beg you, Monseigneur, to give him the post of the tax-collector who is nothing but a dunce. Nevertheless, Monseigneur

---

[6] Author's note: "Copied from an original."

will do well to admit him to retirement, because the peti-
tioner only wants the position of tax-collector and not to
harm him in your mind; it will cost you nothing, Mon-
seigneur, but a stroke of the pen; and the undersigned
petitioner has the pleasure of reminding you that he
found himself guarding His Excellency's door before he
was minister, when he saved him from the Cossacks,
without which Monseigneur would not be His Excellency
today.

The petitioner dies not doubt Monseigneur's senti-
ments of gratitude, with whom he has the honor to be,
etc.

Jacques Bontems.

That done, he assembled the whole sum of his ideas to make a summary of the same genre for the commune's lawsuit, and sent it to one of his former generals, recommending him to pass it on to a Councilor of State "in order," he said, "to have the King issue an immediate decree."

After such dispatches, Jacques Bontems declared to Catherine's father that within a month, he, Bontems, would be appointed tax-collector and that the commune's lawsuit would be settled. The former beadle replied that Catherine would then become his wife, and Catherine uttered a sigh.

Chapter VI
The Pearl Fay

Abel had ended up despairing of ever seeing a fay, and for three or four days he had even put away his books of enchantment, which he knew by heart, having finally resolved not to open them again.

His soul, like those of people who begin to doubt something on which they have founded all their happiness, was delivered to an extremely sweet melancholy; he found a void within himself, thought about Catherine, and he had, in his meditations, all the elements of amour without being amorous. His mental activity dissolved in reveries devoid of object, which plunged him, by virtue of Catherine's absence, into a kind of mental torpor. For several days, his very life was purely animal, and there was only one desire within him: that of having something on to which he could project the mass of sentiment that obsessed him.

Those who have been twenty years old will understand that state of mind perfectly, and those who, at school, are turning these pages furtively, will not take long to discover it.

One evening, after having contemplated the aspect of the sky for a long time, Abel addressed himself to the firmament in his Oriental language. "Clouds," he said, "who often pause on the summits of mountains and deposit the djinni that refresh the earth, send to my cottage some frivolous sprite to instruct me, or prescribe me some difficult task into which I can put all my soul; precipitate me into a lake at the bottom of which I will find lions guarding a young fay sitting on a diamond, asleep for centuries by the order of a cruel enchanter. Star who seems to distil light, descend and give me a talisman for my life. Diving radiance that departs from the bosom of the Queen of the Night, guide me to the land where Farucknaz[7] is to be found, where the roc deploys its wings, where the thousand golden columns of the palaces of the fays rise up."

To Caliban, who was listening to him without understanding, he said: "Oh, soon, perhaps tomorrow, I'll dig up the fireplace, and we'll go somewhere else; for the princes in my tales go out into the world, and that's how they encounter fays, disguised as old beggar-women." He added, however: "But how can I abandon the field where my mother lies? And Catherine, and you, Caliban, who can no longer walk?"

Caliban kissed his hand.

"I want to love!" Abel exclaimed. "I feel something here"—the indicated his heart—"that needs another being than me; my flowers, my cottage and my plants are no longer sufficient for me. I'm alone! O fay of amours, good fay who served the lutin prince so well, come to my aid!"

He went back inside, and lay down sadly on his bed in the laboratory, and did not take long to fall into the

---

[7] Faruck-naz is a character featured in the comic opera *La Petite lampe merveilleuse* [The Marvelous Little Lamp] (1822). Although he had also appeared, as Farucknaze, in at least one earlier stage work based on the story of Aladdin, he is not in Galland's original story, and appears to have been borrowed from an imitation work, *Le Mille et un jours* [The Thousand-and-One Days] (1710-12) by Francois Pétis de la Croix, where he appears as Farrukh-naz.

most profound sleep, as did Caliban, who had a room some distance from his own.

It was around midnight; the most profound silence reigned in nature entire, only troubled by the cool nocturnal breeze that was softly swaying the branches of the trees; a few owls were hooting in the distance; the moon was hidden by large clouds, allowing a profound obscurity to rule.

Abel dreamed that a fay was about to appear; he heard in his dream the enchanting cords of an entirely aerial music, and in the midst of its sounds, he listened with the pure delight of a soul disengaged from the body, to the silvery voice of the fay who surged forth brilliant and clear from the bosom of a cloud of melody, light and dew as blue-tinted as the horizon of the sea.

He woke up with a start, but the sweet music of the dream continued...

Soon, it stopped.

What a spectacle!

In order to give an accurate idea of it, it would be necessary to paint in words the tableau of Endymion:[8] to show Abel, just as handsome as the shepherd beloved by Diana, lying in that attitude, as gracious, and colored, like him, by the amorous glow that announces the goddess—but here, in the laboratory, the goddess had arrived!

---

[8] The theme in question was depicted by various painters, but the particular image that Balzac has in mind is one in the Louvre that he is known to have admired greatly, painted in Rome in 1791 by Anne-Louis Girodet and exhibited at the Salons of 1793 and 1814. Girodet is cited again, by name, later in the story.

Stupefied, Abel has seen, emerging from the fireplace, the object of his dreams, a fay, but the prettiest of fays, the fay of amours!

She is suspended in mid-air in the middle of a cloud of light as white as that of a star and as soft as daylight passed through muslin woven with designs. That light is produced by a bronze lamp, which the fay has left in the fireplace, and which Abel can no longer see. That lamp, antique in form, casts a glow that seems to be a celestial radiance, which illuminates the laboratory. Abel thinks that he is still dreaming; he abandons himself, craning his neck, like a mortal seeing paradise for the first time, to the delight of contemplating the individual whose celestial voice he has just heard.

The song and the music have ceased. From the bosom of her throne of light, the fay seems to be insulting the earth, which she disdains to touch with her snowy feet. She is clad entirely in white, in a white fabric so dazzling that the image Abel had traced of a fay's garments is surpassed.

She had jet-black hair, dotted with pearls whose charming whiteness, softer than that of diamond, made her head resemble a tuft of verdure charged with a thousand dewdrops.

A girdle of pearls circled a slender, light and voluptuous waist; a pearl necklace with fifteen rows was only distinguished with difficulty by Abel, because it seemed to be confused with the fay's skin, so white was she; on her polished arms, delicate and satined, pearl bracelets gleamed; and her dress was embroidered with pearls. She was holding a wand of mother-of-pearl, and from the summit of her head a veil hung down at the back, so light that it seemed to be woven from the wind by the zephyrs themselves. That veil, milk-white, formed in its play a kind of cloud, in the bosom of which she was seated.

That daughter of the air was petite, dainty, lively and light, but nothing can give an idea of her face, the finest effort of nature. It contained all characters: kindness alloyed with gentle pride, grandeur, attraction, amour, grace, and the indefinable charm that results from a desire to please. Her keen eyes, full of moist fire, had the dark circle that doubles their gleam, and they had the most astonishing expression of voluptuousness, almost aerial and vaporous, given by a broad, long and beautiful eyelid with long lashes, when it advances over the middle of the eye and seems to hide the pupil, in which all the burning fire of amour is visible.

Her slender nose respired enjoyment; on her flowery cheek the gleam of a shiny apple was resplendent; and her mouth was smiling like an opening rosebud, allowing a glimpse of teeth rivaling the pearls of her attire. Her divine smile announced a thought as pure and fresh as her breath, and the elegant pose of her neck, which rose from the middle of the gracious curve of her shoulders like a milky column, indicated that she had studied majesty in the heavens. Her harmonious breasts, veiled as they were by an airy gauze, were devoured by Abel's charmed gaze; in the silence of the night, he could hear the murmur of those ivory globes.

To see all of that was the affair of a minute; he seemed fearful that his breath might cause the divine apparition to fly away, and he dared not look at the fay, whose eyes seemed to be stars of the heavens.

The fay took pleasure in enjoying Abel's astonishment, and her gaze was one of curious admiration. She lowered and raised her eyes by turns, until Abel, hearing the fay's respiration, finally stopped doubting the reality of the brilliant creature. He prostrated himself, and, raising his angelic face, he said to her with enthusiasm, and with the voice of adoration: "You are doubtless the Pearl Fay?"

She smiled, and nodded her head as a sign of approval. That gentle movement caused a large diamond in the middle of her pure forehead to glitter; Abel thought that the cloud of light trembled spasmodically, describing multiple circles, like the ripples of a stone thrown into limpid water.

"You have heard my voice, then, beautiful Pearl Fay," he continued, with a charming ingenuousness. "Take in your loving hands the reins of my life! Preside over my sentiments; I dedicate myself to you… if, that is, I am worthy of it—but the offering of a pure heart is, I believe, the most beautiful thing there is on the earth. Oh, come to my cottage sometimes; I shall seek tears of repentance for you, if it is your employment to collect them; I shall raise temples and altars to you; I shall live for you…but speak; I tremble that you might only be the daughter of a dream."

Raphael represents to us angels, seraphim, kneeling before the Eternal, and he has assembled human perfection in a posture that, in spite of its humility, shines with grace; their resplendent visages seem to cast a reflection over the earth, which they cover with the thousand curls of their golden hair: such was Abel before his fay.

She admired him, and for a moment her lily complexion became paler and her blush more vivid; her eyes sparkled, and a magical expression strayed over her radiant face. When Abel had finished his plea, she agitated her head gently, and pronounced these words:

"Abel, I shall see whether you are worthy of what you ask; in the meantime, I shall come to slip into your cottage like a moonbeam that spreads a slivery light and shines in the middle of the night. If you merit it, I shall be your friend, your star, and..."

She stopped, as if she were fearful of making too great a promise.

On hearing that angelic voice, which slid into his ear like the last sounds of a harp, and which had the softness, the harmony and the grace of them, Abel was dazed; the impact of that voice went straight to his heart, and he listened to it with his soul, for it appeared to emerge from that of the fay. The lovely music that had preceded the apparition was no sweeter than that soft chord.

"Oh!" he exclaimed. "If, transported on a cloud, I hear the divine tones of the golden harps that, Catherine has told me, the cherubim play before God, I shall not have more pleasure than is given to me by a syllable pronounced by you! The bird that sings before dying, the nightingale, the golden crossbill,[9] and a mother's kiss are no softer. O Pearl Fay, are you not the queen of all the fays, as the pearl is the queen of the ocean?"

The fay smiled, and intoxicated him by means of that smile.

"If I were eternal," he cried, forcefully, "one such smile every thousand years, and I would be happy! Ask for my head, with an executioner and his ax standing by, but smile at me again and I will die content...your smile would smile at me until nightfall; I would prefer death with that memory to life without you!"

"Adieu, Abel!" she said, in a tender voice.

---

[9] The term *loxia d'or* [golden crossbill] does not seem to appear anywhere else than in this work, so Balzac might have improvised it as an alternative designation of the nightingale.

Abel prostrated himself, and when he raised his head, the fay had disappeared as she had come, and although the young man strained his eyes to distinguish the place that she had occupied, he saw, to borrow Milton's admirable expression, nothing but darkness visible, and heard nothing but silence. However, he distinguished in the distance a muffled sound like that of thunder, and in a reawakening of astonishment he ran out of the cottage. He climbed the hill, and toward the forest he perceived a luminous chariot flying away with the rapidity of a storm-cloud.

He went back inside, but could not sleep until daybreak; he could still see the Pearl Fay and her cloud of light; he could hear that soft voice, and threw himself forward as if to seize the luminous foot that he had seen shining in a cothurne of silvery fabric; he rubbed his eyes, but he could not doubt.

In daylight, he had the proof of the celestial apparition; his mother's footstool was in front of the fireplace, and there were a few pearls thereon, detached from the fay's robe. He investigated the hearth, and found at his feet the debris of an enormous bottle that his father had placed on the mantelpiece, on the label of which Abel remembered always have read the first word: *Spirit*...

"That's it," he said to himself. "My father kept the fay enclosed in it, and her term of imprisonment finished last night."

Finally, he went inside the fireplace, and perceived that on one of its sides, his father, when he enlarged it with Caliban, had left a little staircase there, carved into the stone, and he saw more pearls on several of the steps.

Then he ran to wake Caliban and told him about the fay's coming.

Old Caliban rejoiced, and when his young master had finished, he said to him: "Abel, I'm getting old and I'll die soon. It's necessary, in order to avoid the trouble of cultivating the garden, to mill the wheat and sow the vegetables, to ask your fay to have it done by goblins."

"If only she could make you live forever," said Abel. "But fays don't have that power." That point was doubtful, though, and he promised to reopen the *Cabinet des fées* and look for examples. Then Caliban rejoiced, hoping that Abel might find a ticket to eternity for him on some forgotten page.

Abel went out, and the first thing that struck his gaze was a white mass, a hundred paces from the cottage, that he was not accustomed to see there. He remembered that something else had existed in the same place before, but it was only after a full hour of meditation that he remembered that it was the enormous bush that had hidden Catherine the first time she had ventured on to the hill.

He ran to it and discovered that the bush had been burned, uncovering an enormous stone around which it had grown, hiding it from all eyes. The stone was square, and he perceived bizarre characters traced on the table that covered the rustic monument. At the base of the square block was an extraordinarily large and vast flagstone, buried for many years under the ground. The earth had been dug up and the white slab, in the middle of which was a large iron ring, was now freed from everything that had hidden it for an exceedingly a long time, since the bush had been able to grow there.

That rather considerable labor had been done without Abel being able to hear anything, and that reflection made him think that it was a trick of the pretty Pearl Fay, and that the monument and its hieroglyphic characters signified something very important.

He lay down on the ground, and put his ear to the slab. He heard a muffled sound that might have been mistaken for that of goblins, but which was really produced by the same cause that makes the sound of the sea audible in seashells that children put to their ear.

He stood up again and tried to make sense of the characters, but that was impossible, because they were too bizarre, although Abel was able to make out a few figures effaced by the hand of time.

He was still gazing at the singular monument when he heard footfalls as light as those of a phantom. He advanced his head, thinking that it was the fay. He saw Catherine, who, in spite of her chagrin, was coming toward him cheerfully. Abel could not suppress a movement of disappointment on seeing that he was mistaken; that gesture did not escape Catherine's eye.

"What's the matter?" she said to him, trembling like a winter leaf.

"I thought," he replied, with a soft smile that reassured Catherine momentarily, "that it was the fay..."

"What fay?" she said, surprised.

"The Pearl Fay," Abel replied, his eyes sparkling with amour. "Oh, how beautiful she is! Why, what's the matter, Catherine?—you're turning your eyes away."

"Yes," she said, in a stifled voice. "I can't look at yours when they have that expression..." *and it isn't for me*, she thought.

"What's the matter, my little Catherine?" he said, softly. "You're weeping. Are you suffering, then?"

"Oh, yes, I'm suffering!" Catherine sobbed. She turned round and saw tears in his eyes. "You're weeping too," she said—and immediately, her tears seemed to dry up.

"Can I see your pain without feeling it?" Abel replied. "Are you not my sister, since you're the only person who has smiled at me without being my father, my mother or Caliban?"

"Well," said Catherine, hiding her disappointment, "what is this fay?"

Then Abel, with all the fire of youth and all the fire of amour, gave her an animated and brilliant description of the celestial vision that he had had during the night. At every instant, the most energetic phrases of humans that the friction of civilization has not deteriorated, and who remain *new*, arrived on his inflamed lips, and informed only too well the unfortunate Catherine, who was still listening with pleasure to that sentence of death, like a repentant criminal who has need of torture.

"Finally," said Abel, in conclusion, pointing at the heavens, "it's only beyond that iridescent sash that flowers as brilliant live and die; they come from the flower-bed of the gardens of your God, whom I love even more since he has permitted me to see the roses that bloom near his throne, and which bring therefrom a dew of light and perfumes, and charms of which nature down here has no examples. Yes, Catherine, the whiteness of a virgin lily, the thousand colors of the birds of the Orient, the soft song of swans, the odor of amber, the face of Mohammed's houris…assemble all the forces of nature, and the masterpiece would still be beneath her…"

"You love her?" said Catherine, shivering and glimpsing his response.

"I dare not, for fear that my love might tarnish her purity."

"But if she's so beautiful," said Catherine, "what if she doesn't love you?"

"You're provoking too many thoughts!" he said, striking himself over the heart. "I have too many here—they're choking me."

"You'll love her and she'll love you," said Catherine then, dissolving in tears, "for a woman who has seen you could never forget the sweetness of your face."

Having said that, Catherine fled through the brambles, still weeping...but she stopped, came back precipitately, and, sitting beside him on the large stone, she said to him: "Abel, be happy, and I shall be happy..." And she disappeared.

The pensive young man followed her with his eyes. For some time he did not think any more about the Pearl Fay, and he began to recall within himself all of Catherine's speech, gazes and even tones, but vaguely, and with a confused sentiment that he could not explain.

Chapter VII
The Marvelous Lamp

For several hours, Abel's soul lived, in a way, on the memory of the apparition of the Pearl Fay, but after that, he felt a need to see her that resembled hunger. He tried not to go to sleep at night, in order not to lose any of the moments during which the pretty fay might come. He adorned himself carefully, washed his hair in the clear water of the spring, and tried with Caliban to render as white as mountain snow the collar that his mother had embroidered. He plaited the cords by means of which he attached wooden sandals made by Caliban during winter nights, and on which his feet resembled the marble feet of a statue.

One evening, he and Caliban collected a bouquet of roses, and he strewed the petals in the laboratory, which he ornamented with foliage. He swept the chimney through which the little fay had descended, and attached lilac branches to it, in order that she might find a perfumed path.

The following evening, at midnight, the hour that fays—all fays—cherish, because at that moment the amorous stars cast a more vivid gleam and the silence pleases their loving souls, a music of divine sweetness and the pure and tender song of the Pearl Fay alloyed their melody, which seemed to be coming from the clouds, so cautiously and softly did the harmony caress the ear.

Abel suddenly woke up and saw the fay, in the midst of her cortege of light, which extended over the entire laboratory, like the veil of air that can sometimes be seen over the earth on a beautiful spring day when one climbs a mountain and looks down into a valley.

The charming fay was sitting in the worm-eaten armchair and watching her protégé sleep. As soon as Abel opened his eyes she ceased her celestial song and her face took on another expression.

Abel, who had slept fully dressed since the first apparition, got up, and set himself on his knees a few paces from the fay. A moment of silence reigned between them, for she seemed to be taking pleasure in admiring the young man, whose gaze ran over her avidly, as if he were seeing a tenderly beloved friend again after many years.

Finally, he said to her with a charming naivety: "You've doubtless broken the big bottle in which my father had enclosed you?"

"Yes," she said, smiling. "And it's because he took me from the hands of an enchanter, my enemy, that I've sworn to protect you."

"To protect me?" he repeated, slowly, with a tone of regret and a reproachful gaze

"What more do you want?" said the fay, who understood him perfectly well.

"I don't know," he replied; but after a moment of silence and hesitation, he added, with the air of supplication and tender desire that gives so much charm: "I'd like never to leave you! Have you not rendered life insupportable to me? For if I didn't think about you and your image didn't fill my every moment…what would I become? Nothing pleases me now as much as a relationship between my life and you. My soul was full of happiness in picking these roses, because you were to tread on the petals I've spread. Once, I loved flowers, the murmur of our spring, the sight of the valley and that of the sky; today, all that only has charm because I think I hear a voice replying to me; it's an artifice of my soul, which makes me believe that you're listening to me. Go, beautiful fay; you can be in the places where you rest, but I'm certain that you're also here"—and he pointed at his heart.

The fay—for fays are women, after all—listened with pleasure. She showed him the stool with the tip of her wand, as if to tell him to sit down on it. Abel perched on it timidly, while still gazing at the fay. As he sat down, he perceived the beautiful lamp that was burning on the mantelpiece, and for a moment, he considered it with surprise, in silence.

The fay looked at him and seemed to divine his thought; she smiled.

"Beautiful fay," sad Abel, "can you prolong Caliban's existence?"

She shook her head in a sign of refusal, and replied in her soft voice: "We can give or take away life, but God has forbidden us to make it last longer than it should."

"You recognize Catherine's God, then?"

"Who is Catherine!" cried the fay, emerging from the kind of impassivity on which she was striving to remain. "Is she not a young and pretty woman that you love?"

"Oh, no, I don't love her!" Abel retorted, swiftly. "For we laugh together and I take her hand; by her side I feel that I'm entirely myself. In sum, I cherish her like a sister…and she was chagrined the other day, and I wept with her."

"Abel, listen! If you have some request to make of me, speak. I can grant you anything you wish."

78

"I don't want anything for myself," he exclaimed, softly, "for at this moment, I'm happy! But I feel that I'd have pleasure in seeing my father and my tender mother, the Good Fay, again. You must know them; let me enjoy the pleasant sight of them once more."

"I'll have to consult my books," the fay replied, "and if it can be done, I'll show them to you."

"Oh, kind fay!" cried Abel. "I'd also like to see your palace, the place of your habitual residence."

"Why?" she asked.

"Because then," said Abel, "I'd always see you there, and you'd almost never be absent for me."

She seemed touched by that response, and promised Abel to satisfy his desires. She darted a glance of complaisance at him, in which a sentiment even more delicate gleamed, and made a movement as if to withdraw. "Oh, stay!" said Abel, seizing her pretty hand, which she suddenly withdrew.

The poor young man, reading the disdain on the face of the Pearl Fay, thought he had offended her, and he recoiled shamefully, looking at her with the expression of a criminal asking for mercy, and a tear even formed in his fiery eyes.

"Terrible!" he said, in a whisper.

The fay, very emotional, took a step toward him and presented him with her hand, very near his lips, and when Abel deposited a tender and respectful kiss thereon, he felt the gentle hand tremble as it brushed his face.

In that apparition, the fay was already slightly embarrassed; she no longer had on her face the cheerful expression that Abel had noticed the first time; but the splendor of her adornment prevented the chemist's son from perceiving that change.

She looked at the laboratory attentively, especially the clothes of the chemist and his wife, and then she turned to Abel and said: "The dew is about to be distilled over the flowers; dawn is breaking; it's the hour when we disappear. Adieu..."

Then, as light as a cloud, as gracious as an amorous virgin's thought, she seized her brilliant lamp and launched herself into the chimney through which he had arrived, like a young squirrel climbing a branch, balancing lightly and playing with the foliage.

Abel remained utterly nonplussed; that apparition of the fay left something in his soul that was indistinct and vague, like the first light of dawn rising on the horizon over a blue sea. That sentiment was not amour, for Abel, without yet perceiving it, had a soul full of it, and the fay ought to be the object of his first and last amour; but that movement of his pensive soul resembled hope, without being hope itself.

When the fay had gone, he remembered the singular expression on her face, and the uncertainty, even embarrassment, of her gestures and her countenance.

He was plunged in that meditation until broad daylight, and Caliban found him in the same posture as when the fay had disappeared.

"Caliban, she told me that she can't delay the moment of your death, when it arrives."

Caliban looked at the ground sadly, and when he raised his head again, Abel perceived a large tear trickling through the old man's wrinkles.

"How can I leave you, Abel? But you'll put me with your father, won't you?"

Abel promised him that.

A few days later, the fay appeared to him again, and came to warn him that it was necessary to resolve himself to running the greatest dangers in order to reach the palace where she lived. Abel replied that presenting him with such a prospect was fulfilling his desires.

Then the fay gave him her nacre wand, which, for this time only, would obey the orders he intimated to it, and she said to him, in a voice full of charm: "Abel, tomorrow, when the chariot of the night has traveled the air and you hear midnight chime on the village clock, strike the stone a hundred paces from your cottage with the wand; it will rise up and open a gulf into which it is necessary to hurl yourself; when you have descended, you must march until you see the light of my castle; it will only be visible to you."

The fay disappeared, as usual, leaving him the wand. He never stopped kissing it, thinking that the fay's hand had touched it. He did not know what to do with it; he put it down in one place, and then another, going away and coming back to look at it, as if it were the fay herself.

In the times when Napoléon governed Europe with a bold hand, and appeared to people to be surrounded by a majestic splendor, he confided his portfolio to a young clerk who had to follow the army. The clerk, once he had the portfolio, did not know where to put it; he consulted everyone, and asked them how one carried the portfolio of an Emperor, and what precious substance was contained within it. He never took his eyes off it, as if Napoléon and his genius were contained therein. If someone went past, he looked at it anxiously; if someone came he would show him the portfolio. He told everyone that that he had His Majesty's portfolio at home. In the end, he went mad...

So it was with Abel and the fay, except that his folly was forgivable as amour, whereas the clerk's announced a narrow soul.

Abel waited with a rare impatience for the appointed hour to arrive.

Caliban was absolutely determined to accompany him, and they were both at the stone in question at midnight. When the last stroke of the clock resounded in the air, Abel struck the slab very gently, and it rose up abruptly. The opening immediately vomited a great quantity of flames, and Caliban looked at Abel fearfully; but the intrepid young man, closing his eyes, launched himself into the crater of the little volcano, and Caliban followed him.

They fell on to a soft and flexible substance that received them complaisantly. They heard the stone fall back noisily and found themselves in the most frightful obscurity. Abel stood up, and, putting his hand out in front of him, marched courageously, calling to Caliban; but he could no longer hear the faithful servant. He groped around everywhere trying to find him, but it was in vain. Then he decided to go forward.

He wandered for a long time without encountering any obstacle; the most profound silence reigned, as well as the greatest obscurity.

He traveled for so long, always surrounded by that cortege of terror, that he thought that the night must have ended.

Suddenly, a horrible noise, of which he had never had any idea, resounded like a clap of thunder, and the vault under which he was walking seemed to be shaken by it, and ready to crumble. After the first shudder of involuntary dread that the noise had excited in his body, he resumed marching, but at every moment the noise was repeated, and seemed to be drawing nearer.

Abel stopped, and sat down on a cold stone; there, the most terrible spectacle came to frighten him.

In fact, his eyes were always directed forward by a natural movement, and he was striving to see; that optical tension fatigued him, and it was when that fatigue arrived that the noise ceased, and in the distance, a luminous white dot began to appear. Gradually, that light became alarming and grew, and took on substance—and the substance was that of a giant armed with a club, who approached rapidly and raised the tree-trunk over Abel's head, swinging it.

Abel stood up and ran at the giant, but he heard frightful laughter, and the giant started dancing and retreating, while jumping, still holding the club aloft. Then Abel ran swiftly toward the terrible vision. Just as he was on the point of reaching it, the giant was resolved into a line of extreme thinness, and changed into a serpent, which hissed with all its night, and launched itself instantly upon Abel, who, in that perplexity, tried to strike it with the nacreous wand.

As he touched it with the wand, it recoiled into the most obscure distance, and from there it came back with an awful fury. On the way, it raised itself up on its tail and its head became a human head: a death's head with that fixed and terrible smile, its body swaying on two dry bones, and Abel saw daylight through its empty ribs. He heard the bones creak, and finally, infernal laughter burst forth that chilled him with terror.

At that instant, the fay and all her magical brightness presented herself to his imagination; he closed his eyes and ran with a terrible strength and energy, and when he was weary, he sat down, opened his eyes, and could no longer see anything. He got up, and continued his route. Soon he perceived a soft light at the end of the tunnel through which he had just traveled, and when he reached it, he saw that it was the reflection of the waters of a lake, which was reflecting a multitude of gleams.

In fact, he found himself in a grotto covered with seashells, some rarer than others. That grotto, where nacre was predominant, was the extremity of a limpid lake, surrounded on all sides by luminous trees. A gilded boat was floating in front of the bold young man, who immediately leapt into it, and tried to guide it toward a magnificent Chinese pavilion that he was seeing for the first time in reality.

As soon as he was in the boat, from both sides of the shore, a soft music spread through the air, the most divine sounds; and when the music fell silent, a silvery voice sang a hymn in Abel's honor.

As for him, he enjoyed the most magnificent spectacle that could flatter his marvel-loving soul; he was sailing on a lake in the midst of an ocean of light, which effaced the glimmer of the stars of a sky as pure as the water that caressed the boat with luminous waves. He saw a Chinese pavilion rising up from the bosom of the waters, and every angle and point was garnished with a pearl as large as an egg, and contained a light that, through the oriental envelope, cast a glow as mysterious glow as the fay of the place. The waters appeared to fade away beneath the divine pavilion, through the windows of which he perceived figures moving and dancing like sylphs.

When his boat reached the pavilion, he heard a delightful music and the joyful cries of a troop of fays that were dancing. He stepped out, and suddenly, two tall and strong strangers took hold of him, threw him into a kind of box and carried him off with extreme rapidity. He tried to break the crate in which he was contained, but the bursts of laughter that followed his vain efforts reminded him that human strength was futile against the enchantments of fays.

Finally, the same noise that he had heard during his difficult journey became audible; his prison seemed to shatter, and he found himself alone in the middle of a white cloud and an agreeable odor, in a place that resembled, so far as he could imagine it, the palace of a fay.

It was a circular space; the cupola was supported by thirty columns of white marble, and the interval between each pair of columns was garnished with a precious red fabric attached by lions' claws to the frieze. The parquet, composed of precious species of wood, formed the most ingenious designs; a chandelier, which he thought made of diamond, hung from the middle of the vault, which seemed to him to be a sky, so skillfully was it painted; and the chandelier emitted fires whose glare he could not sustain.

From the bosom of three golden tripods, the sweetest perfumes were exhaled. All around the marvelous room ran a divan, where there were crimson cushions in profusion, and the richness of the woodwork was further augmented by gilding and gemstones. Between each pair of columns stood a bonze pedestal, on which he saw the most beautiful statues in honor of the most celebrated fays. He read the names thereon: the fay Urgelle; the fay Gentille; the Fay of the Waters, etc.[10]

---

[10] *La Fée Urgèle* (1765) is a comic opera with music by Egidio Duni and a libretto by Charles-Simon Favart, based on Voltaire's *Ce qui plait aux dames*, which was itself based of

At first, in his surprise, he did not perceive an open door, and it required him to hear a well-known cherished voice in the next room for him to rush in there immediately...

Another astonishment!

He entered the place where the fay lived. The light came from on high, but it was veiled by an immense ceiling composed of a fabric as white as snow, and folded with a thousand pleats, so that the daylight had a soft whiteness like the fay herself.

That divine redoubt was square in form. In the four corners, crystal pedestals—into the middle of which the fay had poured silver, which gave them a soft gleam—supported cassolettes, which exhaled the sweetest perfumes. Once Abel was inside he could no longer perceive the door, because the walls—if they were walls—were coated with a precious mat white substance with large nacreous seashells, artistically posed, the brilliant ridges of which, changing color and admirably imitated, decorated the fay's boudoir. The base of each shell contained a seed-pearl, and the plinth from the top to the bottom of the apartment was decorated by a girdle of pearls half a foot wide. The seashells stood out, by virtue of the brilliant white of their nacre, from the background, which was a mat white, almost blue-tinted.

Chaucer's "Wife of Bath's Tale." The alternative spelling employed here was used in English translations. Urgèle was featured in later mock-folkloristic stories by other French writers, including Catulle Mendès. Gentille is featured in Madame d'Aulnoy's "Le Prince Lutin." The phrase "fée des eaux" [Fay of the Waters] was commonly used as a generic term for water-sprites,

All the items of furniture, instead of wood, were made of nacre and enriched with designs in mat silver; their fabric was the most brilliant satin, embroidered with pearls figured by the design. Everywhere, delicate white flowers spread their odor of jasmine, orange-blossom and myrtle. In the middle of the room, a vast sculpted alabaster basin contained an amour blowing into a shell, limpid water springing half way up to the height of the apartment, and then escaping via the marble column on which the basin was set. That murmuring water refreshed the air and encouraged reverie.

Finally, on a silver platform at the back of that cloud of whiteness, Abel, dazed by the search, perceived the fay lying majestically in the middle of a bed of dew, as white as the fabric on which she lay. A profusion of pearls, sown into everything that she used, indicated the profession of the Pearl Fay, and her beauty was so true, so brilliant, that as soon as one looked at her, the magnificence of the place disappeared, and one no longer saw anything but her. On a mat silver night-table the beautiful bronze lamp cast a mysteriously soft glow, only providing the light necessary to perceive the beauty of the place, which too bright a light would have rendered fatiguing for the eyes.

The pearl and the white were a combination of candor and mystery that fostered amour like the light of the stars. There is an expertise and a purity in the color that renders it the favorite of all loving and gracious souls, Venus emerged from the bosom of the ocean, but before that, she had emerged from a pearl; for a pearl had to be her cradle, as the soul of a young virgin has to be that of amour. Amour itself is born of the dew in the chalice of a virginal lily. Finally, white without brightness is the friend of the unfortunate; does not the melancholy of the half-tender, half-bitter smile often gaze at the mass of light that forms the white radiance that the chaste goddess of the night sends to the earth? So, in that redoubt of softness, Abel sensed amour taking possession of all his faculties.

The pretty fay got up and ran toward Abel. He did not hear the sound of her footfalls, for she was moving over a snow-white carpet. In the end, he was plunged in such ecstasy that he could not pronounce a single word. He contemplated the fay, fell to his knees, placed his amorous head on the feet of the goddess, and covered them with kisses. The curls of his beautiful hair caressed the fay's feet. She enjoyed his astonishment with an indescribable pleasure.

"Come on, get up," she said, the sound of her voice charming, "and don't be foolish. In truth, fay as I am, I blush for you..."

It Abel had been able to see the color that covered the fay's face he would have been at the peak of his joy. She drew the young man to a white satin sofa; they sat down there together, and the fay, taking back her wand, rapped three times on the night-table.

Suddenly, an ethereal music filled the air with divine sounds. In his ecstasy, Abel seized the fay's hand; they remained side by side for as long as the music went on, and poor Abel, intoxicated by amour, confounded his soul with that of the goddess. His eyes came perpetually to die in the eyes of his companion, who was not at all displeased by that mute homage, and even appeared to take pleasure in it.

Finally, at a moment when three divine voices were singing, in an unknown language, a piece whose notes seemed infused with amour, Abel and the fay were squeezing one another's hands, blushing together, and their hearts were beating in unison; then, gradually, the fay withdrew her hand, and Abel thought he had lost everything when he could no longer feel the delicate fingers of the angel of amour and beauty.

"Why," he said "did I ask to come to this place? I can no longer live on earth, but only in his cloud that you inhabit. My cottage, my garden, my flowers—you have taken them all away, for everything will displease me, and you will have given me nothing!"

"Ingrate!" said the fay, in a tone full of reproach. "Why do you not count the memory of this moment, which, even for me, will not be without charm? Yes, my palace is full...splendid...magnificent; but think, Abel, that the most beautiful habitation of a fay is a pure heart, a heart entirely hers, a great, generous, sensible heart."

Abel looked at her with an expression signifying that he was offering his.

"I hear you," she said, with the delicate smile of an angel opening the door of heaven to a just person, meaning: *Here it is!* "I hear you, Abel...but to communicate with fays and djinn requires vast knowledge that you do not have."

"Can I acquire it?" he asked, swiftly.

"Yes," she replied, "And if you succeed, I shall have a great proof of your...of your...aptitude for science."

"Beautiful fay," said Abel, "you promised to evoke the shade of my father for me. If you have the power to do that..." He set himself on his knees.

The fay stood up, took him by the hand, and, while he was gazing at the white vault shining with a soft brightness, she deposited a kiss on that cherished hand, gathering her soul into the small space that her lips embraced. Abel turned round, but the majestic fay adopted an attitude of cool dignity, and suppressed her pleasure in the utmost depths of her heart. Nonplussed, Abel lowered his gaze.

Then, with her wand, the fay touched a shell, which suddenly vanished; a slight sound caused Abel to look, and he saw his father stimulating his furnace with the bellows, and his mother embroidering his collar; he raised his hand to his neck, to assure himself that that pledge of maternal love was still there, and remained mute with stupor, prey to fear.

He uttered an exclamation, moved forward, putting out his hands, but he was stopped by a substance as cold as ice and as hard as diamond, and he fainted.

When he woke up, he found himself in the fay's arms. She was paler than he was, holding a handkerchief, with which she was wiping his face, and the sweetest perfumes had brought him round. That moment was one of the most beautiful instants of his life; his eyes encountered the anxious eyes of the fay, who was looking at him amorously.

Contemplating that sweet face was a delicious sensation; he did not feel himself yet; he was born to life, with the difference that he knew that he was being born, and that he seemed to be drawing his existence from the fay's eyes. He had no other memory, no perception of himself.

Plunged in a delightful, tranquil, blissful calm, no longer belonging to the earth, he no longer knew who he was, or where he was...no, he was in love, and saw the object of his love smiling at him in the bosom of a cloud of voluptuousness, grace and richness.

The Pearl Fay was coiffed in a manner to realize the idea of an angel, her curls accumulated over her forehead, her gaze compassionate. Abel thought he was in heaven…but when she saw him open his eyes, she left him, and went out.

Abel found himself alone, therefore, in that place of delights, with his ecstasy and his memories. After an amorous reverie, as sweet as the air of the homeland, he perceived the lamp. Then, remembering the story of Aladdin, he conceived the idea of appropriating the fay's—to whom, moreover, he would not be doing any harm *because*, he told himself, *if it's a talisman she won't miss it, and if it's only a lamp, I won't be depriving her of anything very precious.*

What confirmed him in the thought that the lamp was a talisman was its lack of richness, for it was only bronze; then again, a fay ought not to have anything that was not enchanted.

In brief, he stole the lamp, slipped it into his bosom, and promised himself to try it out at the first opportunity.

The fay soon returned, bringing in a precious milk-white vase a beverage that she demanded that Abel drink immediately. While he was drinking she perceived very easily the larceny that he had committed, and, remembering the manner in which he had looked at the lamp, deduced with what intention the theft had been committed.

"Ingrate!" she exclaimed, in a harmonious voice that she tried in vain to render severe. "I heap you with benefits, I satisfy your desires, I do for you what no fay has ever done for anyone, since I have introduced you to my dwelling, at the risk of being reprimanded by all the fays who learn of it—and you take possession of one of my most precious talismans, the one that an enchanter in the great bazaar sold so dearly?"

Abel was on his knees. "Little fay," he said, "don't be angry, or you'll make me perish of dolor."

"Go," she went on. "My only vengeance is to give it to you, telling you what it is necessary to do to make use of it. Rub it beside the great cabalistic stone that is near your cottage; stamp your foot three times on the slab that had to be found there—a precious slab that your father had buried and which I had a great deal of trouble recognizing—and then you can obtain from the djinni of the lamp anything that you desire. Adieu—merit my presence."

She took him by the hand, and, emerging from her mysterious abode, she guided him in darkness through a long tunnel.

The fay pronounced a few words in a strange language; then three men seized him, and placed him on a soft cushion, while covering his eyes with a blindfold, and he felt himself borne away rapidly.

He fell asleep, and after a very long and profound sleep he woke up again, and found himself in bed in his laboratory.

Caliban was by his side, and seemed troubled.

Abel thought he had been dreaming; he rubbed his eyes and looked at his old servant, who was contemplating him with great anxiety.

Chapter VIII
Testing the Lamp

"Isn't this a dream, Caliban? Didn't you come with me into the gulf, yesterday evening?"

"Yesterday evening?" said he old servant. "The day before yesterday, Abel, for it's a day and a night that I've been in terror of your fate."

He continued: "As soon as I had fallen into that vile hole, two strangers grabbed me, and guarded me for some time, after which they reopened the gulf and threw me on to the earth as if it were giving birth to me. I ran to look for you everywhere, but everyone fled from me; finally, I came back this evening and found you asleep."

Abel got up, and when he perceived his lamp, he did not doubt the verity of his adventure.

"Caliban," he exclaimed, "We're the kings of the earth! Look, do you see this lamp? It's a talisman that the fay has given me." And with that, he told him everything that had happened to him.

The wonderstruck Caliban said to Abel that it was necessary to test the lamp right away. They went out immediately and ran to the big stone with a haste that is easily imaginable.

Abel placed himself on the large slab, rubbed the lamp and stamped his left foot three times; then, with a childlike naivety, Caliban and he withdrew and crouched down, trying to look under the stone, if possible. It rose up abruptly. A pretty djinni, wearing a crown of flowers on the head, clad in a white robe garnished with pearls, who was leaning gracefully on a frightful near-naked negro holding a gleaming scimitar, spoke in a harmonious voice, almost as soft as that of the fay.

"Greetings, my adored master, greetings! I am here to listen to your orders, to serve your pleasures, to espouse your hatreds and to obey any order you give, whether it be necessary for me to fly and run before the clouds, drinking space; or, as a sonorous flame, to devour a house; whether I have to flow like a light wave, rise up in a column, change myself into diamonds or become the brilliant carpet on which you tread: I am whatever you wish. What do you desire, master? Speak, speak!"

When the pure song had concluded, Abel and Caliban, gripped by surprise, contemplated the beauty of the group, for the djinni resembled a young woman sitting next to a bronze statue. Abel and Caliban, looking at one another, no longer knew what to ask for.

Eventually, the old servant said to them: "I want our garden to be cared for, for you to do the digging so that I no longer have anything to do but sow and reap; I want the flour ready-milled and as white as milk."

"Yes," said Abel.

The djinni and the negro disappeared immediately, and the stone, which seemed to be alive, closed abruptly, leaving Abel and Caliban in astonishment; they looked sat the slab again, and thought it was a dream. The old servant tried to lift it up by means of the iron ring, but it was impossible. Then they were convinced that the stone was enchanted. Finally, they set about examining the lamp with the same curiosity as a child seeking to break his toy in order to discover what it contains.

Plunged into embarrassment by the multiplicity of his desires, Abel found no other means to put an end to his reverie than thinking about the perfections of the fay, and the celestial charm of the last moments that he had spent by her side.

Amour was burning him entirely, and it was impossible henceforth for him not to mingle the memory of the fay with all his actions, to see her incessantly and relate all his desires to her.

When Caliban came back to the dwelling it was almost dark. He bumped into a heavy object that he found in his path, and when he put his hands on it they sank into it. He pulled them out full of the most beautiful wheat flour that had ever been milled, and he hastened to transport the sack into the cottage. Through the windows of his redoubt he perceived three slaves clad entirely in white, who were briskly digging a square plot of ground by the light of the moon.

He went out and watched them do it with his arms folded, taking a divine pleasure in seeing his work completed as if by enchantment. He approached them and spoke to them, but they did not interrupt themselves, made no movement and did not appear to have heard him. Marveling, Caliban blessed the lamp, the fay, the heavens, and rendered thanks to God that Abel finally had a talisman that would not leave them wanting for anything.

"Well," he said, aloud, "it's forty years that I haven't eaten meat and made a meal of it; I'll have to ask for a splendid one tomorrow morning."

Abel was outside; the moon cast a sash of light over the valley that invited meditation. At the bottom of the hill he heard a sad and melancholy voice modulating the most moving plaints. That hymn of suffering, which resounded in the midst of the most solemn silence, impressed him forcefully.

There are unhappy people in this valley, he said to himself, *and I can help them.*

He advanced, and tried to see the woman who was singing so sadly. He perceived a figure moving slowly among the sonorous poplars that bordered the banks of the stream. She was like the wandering shade of a mortal who has not obtained earth over her abandoned remains.[11] Her movements had the indecisive randomness of a person to whom everything is indifferent, because her heart is full of a single idea, a single desire. She seemed to be roaming the valley in order to bid it adieu.

At that moment, a melodious respiration announced Catherine. Abel ran to meet her and, showing her his lamp, he said to her, joyfully: "Ask me anything you wish, Catherine; this precious talisman that I possess will grant your wishes."

"Oh," she said, "what I desire can never come from that metal lamp."

"Yes, my little Catherine."

Then he told her his latest adventure, and the poor peasant girl had a heart filled with bile on listening to the expressions of amour that Abel employed.

"Oh, Catherine," he said, as he concluded, "the misfortune about which you spoke to me, of loving without being loved, I have felt that cruel suffering. How can one say to a fay: 'I love you!' How can one dare to look at her with that thought, which must be legible in one's face..."

---

[11] Author's note: "The ancients believed, and many people still believe, that the dead who are not buried lament for a long time, because they cannot enter heaven."

96

"Why don't you love instead," said Catherine, sharply, "a young woman who would carry you in her heart, and for whom you are what the fay is to you…?"

She stopped, and silence ranged throughout nature. After a few moments, the young woman who was wandering in the valley gave voice to her song of despair; it said that she loved in vain. Those tones seemed prophetic to Catherine; she wept.

"Catherine!" exclaimed Abel. "Oh, you're hiding some chagrin from me! That's bad, for now I can do anything for your happiness."

"I was thinking," she said, making an effort to control herself, "about poor Juliette, whom I've just heard."

"What? That's her?" Abel replied. "Oh, ask her to come, Catherine, and my lamp will remove all the obstacles that separate her from Antoine."

Catherine ran through the bushes, admiring the good heart of her beloved, without understanding how he would render Juliette happy. But she went, she ran, she flew, for she and Juliette were plunged in the same unhappiness, and there was mention of helping her sister in amorous misery.

Juliette arrived; she was beautiful but pale, and on her face, which respired the tomb, traces were visible that declared that she had been all kindness and gaiety before love had illuminated the fire shining in her sunken eyes. She sat down in a fashion to indicate immediately that everything was indifferent to her, and her gaze announced a vague anxiety for a treasure that did not belong to her.

Juliette, no longer herself, was living elsewhere, and there, where she posed with grace, there as only her elegant and pure form, for her soul was still voyaging. Catherine, contemplating her, read her own future. When she told Juliette that the young man had the power to make her Antoine's wife, a glimmer of hope wandered over her face, and modified it like the errant sparks that run through the ashes of a burning piece of paper.

She turned her death-filled eyes toward Abel, but she did not perceive his rare beauty, because someone else had given her another ideal type, and she replied slowly, looking at the ground: "The grave will be my nuptial bed, and the hymns of the church in mourning will be my wedding march. Antoine! Antoine..." Then she contemplated the vault of the heavens and the stars, the mantle of azure and the valley. "Adieu, adieu." Her hair was loose, and she resembled Ariadne abandoned—but an Ariadne ready to perish.

"Catherine," said Abel, "what is necessary to enable her to marry the man she loves?"

"I imagine," she replied, "that thirty thousand francs would remove all the obstacles."

Abel stamped three times and rubbed the lamp. When the djinni had sung his song of obedience, and plunged Catherine and Juliette into astonishment, Abel asked for thirty thousand francs.

"Before your arteries have pulsed ten times," replied the djinni, "you shall have what you desire." He disappeared, and reappeared immediately; he set one knee on the ground and indicated a large bag of gold, which the negro dropped on the ground. They waited for Abel to give the order to withdraw, and soon departed, singing

An emanation of extraordinary sweetness filled the air with its perfume. Catherine and Juliette, astounded, stood there in a daze, looking alternately at Abel, his lamp and the stone—but at Abel longer than the others, for he seemed to them, by virtue of his attitude, an angel descended from the heavens.

Juliette, the fortunate Juliette, contemplated him with an effusion of the heart that made her face shine with the intoxicating joy that fortunate amour gives, and immediately, her initial grace and gaiety reappeared in her stance and her movements.

"If you're a man," she said, with a delicate smile, "you will be almost a rival of Antoine in my soul; your place will always be marked in the corner of the hearth in our cottage, and no one else will take it."

"Now you're happy!" Catherine said to her, sighing.

"Oh yes, very happy!" Juliette replied, turning her gaze to the farm where the man she loved amorously was asleep.

A melancholy smile strayed over Catherine's lips, and she said, with a hint of bitterness: "For women who marry their beloved, virtues are not difficult to practice."

Abel looked at them with a naïve curiosity, and did not understand the thanks of which he was the object, for he experienced a great pleasure, which he felt owed something to Juliette and Catherine.

He took their hands, and pressed them to his heart, which made Catherine shiver, and said to them with the enthusiasm of youth that has something endearing about it, because it emerged direct from the soul: "Oh, you have made me know the pleasure of the fays! Will you bring me all the unfortunate people?"

Juliette promised to come back often to the stone on the hill, and the two young women, lifting up the bag filled with gold, went away, often turning their heads. Abel watched them go down the hill and reach the village.

Chapter IX
The Empire of the Fays

Abel remained plunged for some time in the charming state of mind that follows an extreme pleasure. To have rendered someone happy is an enjoyment that comes from a sixth sense, which not everyone has. Those who have it will understand perfectly what Abel felt, and those who do not would never understand it, even if there were twenty printed pages here explaining it to them.

Abel thought that his dear fay would come that night, but he was mistaken, and spent all the time desiring her, thinking alternately about the enchantments he had overcome, the brilliant lake that he had traversed, and above all, the cradle of nacre in the bosom of which he had admired the Pearl Fay. The pressure of the hand by which they had mutually testified their pleasure was retraced in Abel's imagination with such fidelity that he thought at times that he was still holding the fay's hand.

In the morning, he felt mortally sad; he went to the slab and tried to lift it in order to discover the way to the enchanted palace, but his efforts were futile. He came back to sit on his rustic bench, trying to consume time in order to disguise from himself the interval that separated him from the next night, during which he hoped the fay would reappear. Like the children of nature who only ever have one idea, one desire, and cannot conceive that they might be distracted from it, Abel only wanted one thing and only thought about one thing: his fay.

Suddenly, he heard a celestial voice that was murmuring a song of amour so softly that the air was barely stirred by it. She was there behind him: more tricks!

A simple white robe garnished at the hem by a few pearls; a white satin girdle; white roses in her hair, and pretty white cothurnes made up her attire.

She sat down beside Abel, and before he had pronounced a single word she said to him: "I've come to see you devoid of all my pomp, for you have placed yourself almost at the level of a fay by the use you have made of the talisman." Trembling slightly, she added: "Abel, if genius is the fire and the sublime sound of a beautiful soul, benevolence is the perfume it exhales. Pure benevolence, without any other goal than doing good, is one of the traits of the God to whom fays and humans owe everything." Looking at him, and immediately lowering her eyes, she said: "I'm content."

The delicate smile with which she accompanied her final remark intoxicated poor Abel so much that he could make no reply, and they both remained mute, as if ashamed. The fay especially appeared to be enjoying a sensation long desired; she was contemplating Abel with an air of anxiety that seemed to be saying: *Will he speak to me?* Her eyes radiated desire and amour, and nothing was more attractive than that visage resplendent with grace and tenderness.

"Oh," said Abel, after having admired her covertly, darting one of those oblique glances at her that are so voluptuous, "you can put on the garments of a mortal, but it will always be evident that you're a fay."

"No," she replied, "at this moment, I'm no longer a fay. You can speak to me as your equal, and I have no strength to take offense at what you say."

All of Abel's countenance had already said "I love you," but while thinking it, an indescribable modesty, preventing him from pronouncing that divine statement, which seemed to him a veritable crime—or rather, the fear of offending the fay and learning that she did not share a love so insensate, held his tongue captive. At that moment he was, to a supreme degree, under the influence of that modesty, the prerogative of great souls, which ensures that, at a young age, one can only shiver at the aspect of a youthful beauty, adore her in silence, count the touch of her robe as the greatest of pleasures, and kiss her footprints when she has gone.

The little fay perceived that mute homage of an extreme amour clearly, so she savored it in silence with an inexpressible delight. For who can see oneself reigning despotically over a heart full of love—a heart in which no other object can find room—without an indescribable joy?

"Abel," she said, "You won't see me again for several days, because I'm obliged to go to a great fête, at which many fays and enchanters will be present."

"How beautiful that must be!" Abel exclaimed, "And how I'd like to see such an assembly—in which you would doubtless be the most beautiful!"

"Nothing is simpler," replied the fay, "and if your desire isn't satisfied when I've told you what happens there, I'll take you there one day. Listen to me carefully. At the hour when everything in nature is asleep, the fays and enchanters mount their chariots and arrive, one after another, at the palace of the djinni that is giving the fête; all the fays take care to try to arrive last, in order that her adornment, being seen last, obtains the victory, for fays are singularly intent on making their costume triumph.

"That singular circumstance changes time and its modifications in the Empire of the Fays, for if one is invited to go to the palace at ten o'clock, that signifies midnight, and no one arrives before one o'clock in the morning. The enchanters are all dressed in black, because they think, sagely, that the absence of any color is advantageous to them, because colors are at the moment an object of trouble and confusion in the realm of the fays. Red, blue and white have been successively fashionable, with the consequence that their combination is a subject of scandal, and the present king is a white djinni. The blue djinn are the enemies of the white djinn and the red djinn are even more terrible.

"If the white djinn were not retained by the king of the fays, they would already have put all the blues and reds in bottles; so, in order to avoid disorder, everyone dresses in black, so that one can only recognize them by their language, for each color has its grimoire, its manner of speaking and its habits. The white djinn see everything in rosy shades; the blue djinn see everything blackly; and the red djinn don't see anything at all. For the first, the sight of water that always finds it level is a horrible thing; for the second, the sight of a palace and chariot containing djinn who don't refer to themselves simply as djinn, and live on a *de*, is a fatal scene; finally, the third class of djinn would like to break all the enchanters' wands and turn everything upside down, in order to give every fay a equal power; those sorts of djinn all have a banner, and a slogan to which they attach their actions and thoughts, and don't perceive that they all want to same thing under different names.

"There are also many quartered djinn, who are all colors, but their dictionary is so short and their belly so fat, since it contains all shades, that they have little esteem, for they're always in favor of the strongest. It's the bottom of the barrel of power that the enchanters are disputing. They all say the same thing, and assemble at the statues in the gardens, which all the property-owners have, so that they're recognized immediately, all the more so as they have no wand, because their power is subordinate to that of the daylight enchanter, which means that they're always hungry, and always have the appearance of eating for the hunger to come, because they're afraid that one day, one of the three parties will be strong enough, and, having no more need of them, might be seen for what they are—which is to say, horses for any saddles, sacks for any grain, mobile consciences—and might be sent to reign in the air and direct fleeting clouds or group mists around the sun, or, better still, supervise the colors of the rainbow.

"There are enchanters of all these classes who come to these gatherings with a multitude of fays, and this is what happens there. When the old fays arrive, they're placed on benches of honor along the walls, and there they're content to watch what happens without taking part in it, because they're old; but their tongue, having inherited all the activity of their body, compensates them by gossiping about the young fays and the enchanters. If a djinni looks too much at a little fay they cry scandal, and the entire tapestry stirs as if it were a matter of a revolution. As everything has been anticipated, the old fays have little pieces of wood garnished with satin, and when they get bored they extend the satin in front of their faces and yawn silently, for it's forbidden in the Empire of the Fays to open one's mouth other than to speak.

"The old fays also guard the places and the mantles of the young, and render them a thousand petty services, like revealing to the enchanters that some fay who seems to them to be as straight as a reed only achieves that delightful figure by rounding herself out with cleverly-positioned cushions. They can spot, from a league away, fays who put a red substance on their overly pale lips, and tell the enchanters to beware of kissing them, for fear of carrying their colors away. They divine the padding that a fay puts in her shoes when one is too short, and lay bare all the tricks that they once practiced.

"Then the young fays get their revenge by stepping on the tails of little dogs, of which the old fays are very fond. In fact, if a dog dies, they keep its portrait in a locket, like that of a cherished lover. Or, again, the young fays mock the pretentions of the old—and that, my dear Abel, is one of their greatest amusements.

"The palace is illuminated by artificial fires, reproduced by diamonds, and it is ornamented with pebbles crushed and powdered in great mirrors, in order that a fay, in passing by, can see whether her costume is disordered, or make a sign to some enchanter or other, having understood, by some sign or other, that he wants to talk to her.

"Then, when almost everyone has arrived, each enchanter takes a fay, and they all start dancing to the sounds of an orchestra, traversing the principal hall of the palace in a more or less pretty fashion, tracing bizarre figures with their dancing to see who can jump, dance, traverse and turn with the most skill. Finally, when everyone is leaping, dancing and laughing, more serious affairs are treated. A djinni who leaps is much more tractable; one obtains what one wants from him much more easily.

"If one of you came in then, without hearing the music, he would see the most singular spectacle in the world: he would see two hundred divinities, almost all in the air, plying their feet without any goal, without wanting to get anywhere, and moving their heads, their eyes and their tongues at random. On that stupid momentary feast, for that aerial dance, the most sumptuous costumes are lavished, when their price could relieve thousands of unfortunates.

"Finally, the enchanters and the old fays, all of whose joints are stiff, whose sinews are too hard, and who, in consequence, can no longer leap, go into other rooms. There, they all stand in front of a table, occupied in watching two enchanters holding little pieces of cardboard; that is their most sublime occupation, their most cherished language, their favorite amusement, their dream, their unique thought.

"In fact, throughout the time that the fête lasts, the room where the green tables and the cards are, never empties; all the djinn, male and female, blue white or red—for in that occupation all ranks, opinions and distinctions disappear—never take their eyes off the little colored cards that go back and forth; and if one of you, wanting to take advantage of the admirable discourses that the greatest of enchanters ought to make when they are assembled, on listening, he would hear: 'Four to five, four to four, three to one, one, two, three, one to four, four to nothing, three to nothing, won, sunk, no more bets, twenty francs to win, a dancer, the king, the trick, the royal fork, etc.' Those words and those cards are so attractive that the fays and djinn forget to eat and drink, and if the room collapsed they would not even notice it until someone told them that the palace had 'played its hand.'[12]

"When the fays and the djinn are weary of traversing the enchanter's reception rooms in every direction, and they see the dawn expand its freshness, they go away, without saying anything to the enchanter who has received them, as if they had not even sought him out on arriving. It often happens that an enchanter who gives a fête does not even know who the djinn he has seen are.

"Such is the principal amusement of fays; it is one of their favorite pleasures, for the duration of which they forget the earth and its inhabitants, the unfortunate, the ill, everything, and even glory at these assemblies in speaking in a jocular fashion, in which everything, including the most serious and lamentable things, is presented with witty modifications, and assaults are mounted of cruel jests. If an unfortunate on earth is ruined, and a pretty little fay is told, she replies: 'He won't ride in a carriage anymore!' If famine desolates a region, and there is no grain with which to make bread, they will say: 'Let them eat cake!'"

"I'd rather help some Juliette with my lamp than savor those pleasures," said Abel.

"Dear child," exclaimed the fay, "you're lucky to be alone in this little cottage, for the empire of the fays has many other singularities, which I'll explain to you some day, and our power is sold to us more dearly than you might think."

---

[12] The djinn are playing *écarté*; the simpler English version of the game is not as rich in exotic terminology, so some of the translated terms are not employed therein.

"It is, however," he replied, timidly, "a place such that all cottages are places of suffering when one has seen it..."

"I understand," replied the fay, smiling. "Well, wouldn't you like to accompany me for a moment along this terrestrial path...toward that place?"

He stood up and, taking her by the hand, walked with her toward the forest. Abel's head was full of new ideas, to which the fay's singular story had given birth, so there was silence between the two of them, like a common friend serving as a mediator, and to whom they were confiding their thoughts. At times, Abel looked at his beautiful and genteel companion, covertly, as if he had some secret thought to reveal to her; then he lowered his eyes and dared not speak for fear of offending her. At such times one is more than ever inclined to ask insignificant questions, either to embolden ne to speak or to evade the devouring desire.

"We're going toward the forest," said Abel, "Tell me more, I beg you, about what happens in the empire of the fays, for I'm hungry for your speech; it nourishes me, and I love the sound of your voice as I once loved the sight of my father..."

"Dear child," she replied, with a keen emotion, "the more I introduce you to the usages of the empire of the fays, the more you will find to complain of its inhabitants. For instance, do you think that he marriage of a fay and an enchanter happens as you imagine the union of two beings ought to be made? Let's see, Abel, what do you think about amour? What has it revealed to your pure soul?"

"Oh," said Abel, "amour is the fusion of two souls into one alone; it's a sympathy that unites two hearts to such an extent that one has not a single thought that the other does not have; it's...but no, that sentiment loses in being defined, for I sense something immense that confounds me, and here I understand that human language stops, and that one ought only to speak of it with the soul alone. In sum, I imagine—to try to say something that might express what I think—that once one is in love, amour takes such full possession of us and of nature that there is nothing else but it, heaven and us, as, when one is on the ocean in a boat, there is no longer anything but the celestial vault and the water."

"Well, Abel," said the fay, "in our empire, no one worries about sentiments; as soon as an enchanter has a little fay to be married, one begins by dressing her up a little better than usual, and calculating how many flying dragons the family has in its stables, and how many slaves in the palace, but above all, once examinees with a curious care the weight of the family wand, whether that wand is made of diamond, gold, silver, copper or iron, and what title it has.

"Once these important observations are made the father and mother make their daughter repeated speeches, which amount to this: 'My child, you're eighteen years old—for fays have an age exactly like mortals—and it's shameful not to be married by twenty; try, therefore, to extend your nets and catch a husband, the year might perhaps be good. But given that we have two hippogriffs for our chariot, one slave behind, that our family wand weighs thirty carats, is gold and has a first-rate title, you need an enchanter who has a wand worthy of yours. You will have no virtues, you will be unworthy to live, if you don't find an enchanter who also has a chariot with two hippogriffs. We have three hundred years of antiquity; in the empire of the fays, it's also necessary that your husband be of an enchanter family equal to ours. Refrain, therefore, from ever raising your eyes toward the djinn; walk straight; conserve yourself for the man that pleases you, but who has a fine wand, two fine dragons hitched to his chariot as at least two hundred years of antiquity.'

"With that, one morning or one evening—it doesn't matter which—the father brings by the hand some enchanter or other, and when he has spent an hour or two with his daughter, and has gone, the mother, at a sign from the father, says to the fay: 'My child, that djinni is hunchbacked or sturdy, ugly or handsome—it doesn't matter which—my child, that djinni has four hippogriffs and he possesses a diamond wand; he'll come back tomorrow; try to please him, for that's your husband.'

"Then the little fay, who is curious to know why one marries, does not look twice, and, ignorant of what constitutes happiness or unhappiness, consents because she cannot do otherwise; then, after a fortnight, she has to marry the djinni, solely because he has a diamond wand. She will be happy if the character of the djinni is good, unhappy in the contrary case; that doesn't matter; the wands are of the same genre, and that is the essential thing. So, very often—almost always, in fact—the fays are unhappy...

"Then, in order to avenge themselves, they amuse themselves opposing their husbands; everything that comes from him is always poisoned, simply because it comes from him; if he has good qualities, that's convenient, but there's always something, some vice, that spoils them, and that vice always comes down to this: he's a husband.

"The enchanter, for his part, cannot love his fay, because she is always the same fay, and does not have the talent, as some fays have, of metamorphosing in a thousand ways, with the result that they offer a thousand fays in one; so, the majority of marriages are unhappy..."

"What about you?" asked Abel, immediately. "Are you happy or unhappy? You have a beautiful wand—from whom did you get it?"

"From an enchanter who was very dear to me....," she said, then, and tears came to her eyes. "Abel, I have been married, my enchanter is dead, and I have been very unhappy! One day I shall tell you about my misfortune; let it suffice for you to know that I am free, and one of the most powerful and richest of all the fays..."

They were on the edge of the forest; there, the Pearl Fay gently disengaged the arm that Abel was holding, and, by means of a gesture, forbade him to follow her. Soon, she disappeared, leaving the young man prey to his delirium.

In fact, he had just seen the Pearl Fay, during that morning, perhaps even more beautiful than when she arrived by night, surrounded by the prestige of her power. She had shown herself in the simplest and most elegant costume; she had sparkled with intelligence and grace; her slender and delicate figure, the pure beauty of her face and the charm of her tender soul had all been deployed with a vivacity and a plenitude that had intoxicated him.

"Oh, I love her!" he cried, after having listened for a long time to the chariot that was carrying the fay away. *Will I ever be sure that my homage will not displease her? Alas, will I ever have the purity of soul, of desire and of thought worthy of that heavenly creature? All the softness of nature is in her gaze and her eyes seem to be a frail veil through which one can perceive her soul. What can I do to merit her? Then, she might love me!*

Such were his thoughts as he returned slowly to the cottage; the memory of that charming morning was engraved eternally in his heart, for he would always remember the fay's merest words and slightest gestures, as well as the aspect that the sky presented during their conversation. That sweet remembrance is one of the attributes of amour.

As he approached his cottage, Abel heard cries of immoderate joy, bursts of laughter and a sound of bottles and plates. He hastened to go in through the garden hedge, and found Caliban sitting on a stool with his elbows on a table covered with the debris of a host of dishes. The old servant was drunk; he was holding a bottle in one hand and a glass in the other, and he was singing at the top of his voice.

All that Abel could get out of him was to learn that in the morning he had gone to rub the lamp at the enchanted stone, that he had asked the djinni for a good feast, which had been brought and served in the space of two hours by the fay's servants.

Abel left poor Caliban with his bottles, and the old servant, in losing his reason, did not lose very much.

Chapter X
Catherine

While these things were happening at the chemist's cottage, the village was in revolution, and one can only give the reader a complete image of it by introducing the reader into the house of Monsieur Grandvani, the father of the lovely Catherine.

Our painters often make interiors seductive in their admirable canvases; why should humble prose not be able to approach the effect the effect produced by the brush, and trace lines that the eye of the soul can color with the most vivid hues? The Muses are sisters, and hence rivals.

Picture, then, that village, with only one street, and that not very straight, and thus obedient to the law that wants all human things to go awry. The cottages each had their little garden, their courtyard full of straw, the humble dwelling of a donkey or fecund chickens, and containing laborious inhabitants, poor but having a sum of happiness and unhappiness similar to that of city-dwellers, except that their affections were directed toward simpler objects.

Half way along the street stood the house of the Lord, little different from those of the peasants, but endowed with a harmonious bell, a veridical historian that presided over life and death as well as all the occupations of the inhabitants. In front of the church, the God of which was simple and devoid of ostentation, a square surrounded by large elms saw every Sunday the frolics of a young troop of dancers, and heard the coarse laughter excited by wine, the sole amour of old men; and there, renown and public opinion set up their stalls, exactly as elsewhere, except that they were made of wood that still had its bark.

On that square there was one house slightly less humble than the others; it had a first floor ornamented by three casements with green shutters; the door was painted with a very particular care, and the local Girodet had been able to find two shades of gray to depict the moldings. Finally, above the door he had written *Mairie*, without any spelling mistakes, because he had painted the sacramental word with the aid of the *Bulletin des lois*. To either side of the door lived a rose-bush surrounded by a little green trellis, and those bushes bore tufts at their head garnished with roses, all the way to the shutters of the first floor room inhabited by the charming Catherine—for that house is her father's. It is the only one, except for the curé's, to be covered with red tiles, and which has a grain-loft where the cambric that lifted Catherine's bosom can be laid out and dried, along with the cravat from which the Maire had made his sash.

On entering the house, one recognizes immediately the presence of a daughter, for the most careful cleanliness is the only thing that decorates the antique staircase that is offered to the gaze.

To one side is the kitchen, with a large fireplace, terracotta ovens with tiles always brown but clean: the bread-bin, the food cupboard and the shiny table-top are all tidy, and there is not a single spider to listen to the melancholy sound of the dripping water escaping slowly from the osier fountain that garnishes one of the corners.

To the other side is Grandvani's room; at the back, one sees the bed with antique twisted posts and green serge curtains. The floor has walnut joists and the tiles are clean and always scrubbed. On the Portland stone fireplace there is a mirror, on one side of which hangs a calendar, and on the other a poor print representing *The Death of Poor Credit*, killed by painters, musicians, authors, actors and speculators, with a long story commenting on that tragic adventure, but the designer, unable to represent governments in material form because they change too frequently, has forgotten those assassins of poor Credit.

Facing the fireplace is a long box that contains in its slender body the pendulum of a chiming clock, surmounted by the statue of an animal whose gilt is effaced. The paper that decorates the wall is charged with birds that are singing while looking at you incessantly, and seem as if they have been petrified, because they remain eternally in the same place, always looking at you with the same gaze, which sovereigns and friends do not have.

The window is ornamented by two printed cotton curtains with a thousand flowers, lined with calico. There, a chair permanently set before a small table, like a sewing-table, on which are scissors, a thimble, thread, wax, Grandvani's jacket and a half-embroidered collerette, inform you that this is Catherine's habitual station. It is there that she sits, because outside she can see, through the window, everything that is happening in the square.

Before knowing Abel, she saw in the distance the sergeant, Jacques Bontems coming, and her father knew when he was approaching on seeing Catherine come to embrace him, for she dared not admit that she ran to look at herself in the mirror, in order to assure herself that her headscarf was straight, her face pleasant and the curls of hair neatly positioned. She blushed, listened, and ran to open the door after having placed a chair beside her father.

As for Grandvani, he was in the corner of his hearth, beside his bed, in a large velvet winged armchair from Utrecht, the original color of which could no longer be distinguished, although it was a safe bet that it had once been yellow, given that it was now so worn that it was almost white, and only yellow turns white.

The old man was always in black knee-breeches, black stockings, with a blue coat with big metal buttons sculpted in facets, wearing a round gray bonnet like those worn by diligence conductors. The cheerful fellow, a trifle miserly, loving wine but loving his daughter more, acted in the locale whose cock he was like the autocrats of the Orient—which is to say that he rarely went out, and his favorite occupations were chatting and reading. He had beside him a table on which lay the mayoral registers, an inkwell, a few quills, the seal—the sign of his power—and finally, a shelf of stamps, plus the laws and edicts that were sent to him, and from which he drew the principles of his conduct, while seeking to divine that of the government—research in which he was powerfully aided by Jacques Bontems, which ensured that they both went astray in that inextricable labyrinth.

Most often, silence reigned, and the pendulum of the clock was alone in speaking, especially since Catherine had fallen in love with Abel.

The furniture of that room was becoming: a walnut tale that had served for more than one feast, chairs garnished with printed cotton cushions, antique armchairs, and, in front of the mirror on the mantelpiece, a plaster virgin holding her infant, with carmine-tinted cheeks. A plaster portrait of the King and a bust of Bonaparte—the latter in the cupboard—completed the furniture of that abode of peace and tranquility.

It was before that hearth and before Grandvani that all the quarrels of the village were settled; he was its king, and he had no other ministers than the curé and the sergeant: all people of good composition, having no liking for reactions, interventions, revolutions, destitutions, purges or conspiracies, veritable or otherwise.

That haven of peace thus respired a rural ease, and a calm that pleased the soul; but it would have seemed like paradise to anyone who saw the charming Catherine sitting in her chair, her face illuminated by daylight, her agile hand plying a needle, in a mild reverie, and looking at her father with a meek and calm affection, a pure pleasure, sometimes pushing the curls of her hair away from her pale forehead rich in innocence, and getting up to chase away a few specks of dust—the only thing in the world she could hate.

So she had been, once: naïve, cheerful, with a keen gaze, but ignorant and chaste, listening to everything with a virginal curiosity, and smiling at what she did not understand; but at the moment we are about to describe, although the furniture, the room, the atmosphere and the worthy Grandvani have not changed at all, the poor child is astonishing.

A lamp is set on the mantelpiece. Grandvani is half-asleep in his armchair, and Catherine is embroidering a muslin headscarf by the ruddy light of the nocturnal star that is shining in that modest room. Françoise, the domestic, is in a corner turning her spinning-wheel and spinning in silence.

Poor Catherine, who once chatted randomly about what was happening in the village and filled, for her father, the role of a gazette, preventing him from going to

117

sleep after dinner, is mute, even after the event that is astonishing the village, news of which has not yet crossed the threshold of the Maire's house. However, Catherine knows the fact, since she was one of its actors, and has seen with her own eyes that which is stupefying the entire village. Yes, but Catherine is mute, she is letting her father sleep, who has been trying for a long time to hold on to the snuff-box that has finally slipped from his fingers. Catherine is plying her needle slowly; she often stops, raises her eyes, thinks she sees a cherished image, and sighs in that contemplation.

The poor child is in love, in love with her soul; her senses have nothing to do with it; she wants to hear forever the soft voice that speaks of enchantment and fays; she would like to mingle, by means of a gaze, her soul with that of the man who seems to her to be all beauty, all love.

Silence reigns so well in the room that one can count the movements of the clock and Françoise's spinning-wheel. Suddenly, someone knocks on the door, and several voices are heard, that of Jacques Bontems among them.

Catherine does not get up precipitately; it is no longer her who runs to open the door; she no longer looks in the mirror framed in sculpted black wood; no, she remains motionless, tears ready to invade the crystal limpidity of her amorous eyes, and it is Françoise who gets up and runs to open the door.

At that noise, Grandvani wakes up.

Antoine's father and the sergeant come in, and their countenances announce that something extraordinary has happened.

"Bonjour, Monsieur le Maire," said the stout farmer, sitting down next to Grandvani

"Is all well, Père Grandvani?" says the cavalry sergeant, shaking the hand of Catherine's father, and he adds, addressing the young woman: "And you, Mademoiselle, you no longer recognize your friends, since, for some time, you no longer come to open up…because I could hear through the door when it was you; you sang the refrain of a song so prettily!"

Catherine made no reply and Jacques Bontems looked at her with astonishment.

"Monsieur le Maire," said the stout farmer, turning his hat in his hands, "I've come for an affair of consequence. Mademoiselle Catherine has doubtless talked to you about it, for there isn't a child in the village who hasn't heard about it."

"What is it, then?" Grandvani replied. "No, I don't know anything, Françoise, bring us a bottle of wine; that will rinse our throats."

"And the dust will vanish in speech," added the cuirassier.

"Can you imagine," continued the farmer, "that that little Juliette, who wants to marry my son, came home last night with thirty thousand francs in gold?"

"Bah!" said Grandvani, opening his eyes wide. "Where did she get them, then?"

"Ah, that's it!" said Jacques Bontems. "There's those who say that she, who hadn't got a sou yesterday, and had the devil in her body for Antoine, must have robbed someone! For a girl in love in worse than a regiment of grenadiers…"

At this point, Catherine blushed and abruptly interrupted the cuirassier, crying: "Get away! It's wicked to accuse poor Juliette of such an infamous action! She, who is so gentle, so loving, so pretty, how can you?

"Ah!" said the farmer. "You know something about it; for the whole village knows that you helped her to carry the bag of gold home."

"Certainly," said Catherine.

"Oh, Père Grandvani," cried the cuirassier, "look at your daughter! She has a red footprint over her face, as if an English regiment had galloped over it."

Grandvani looked at his daughter, and said to her in a tone that he tried to render severe: "Catherine, what does this mystery signify? What has happened, then? Was it you who opened the door so quietly at ten o'clock? I thought it was Françoise! And I was already wondering who her lover could be."

"Yes, father, it was me..."

At those words, Grandvani put his glass down on the table, Françoise quit her spinning-wheel, the sergeant caressed his moustache, the farmer stopped rotating his hat, and all four of them remained motionless, their eyes fixed on Catherine, open-mouthed; and the poor child, looking at the farmer, said to him:

"So, Père Verniaud, you're going to make your son happy, since Juliette is rich, and you've come here to fulfill the formalities."

"No, Mademoiselle," said the farmer. "So long as I don't know the source from which Juliette obtained her thirty thousand francs, I won't budge."

"Go on, daughter, tell us where they came from."

Then Catherine blushing, over and over again, recounted the apparition of the djinni of the lamp, as soon as a handsome young man rubbed it and stamped on the enchanted stone. She told them everything she knew about the chemist's son, and her naïve eulogies, her candor, ignited the bile of Jacques Bontems, who cried:

"Name of the Devil, I can see it clearly! That fine conscript there is some villain who's only paying her for what he took. By the bowl of my pipe and a thousand bombs, you won't be the grandfather of your son's child, Père Verniaud, for this business hides some farce, and I tell you that it's a tale that Mademoiselle Catherine is giving us. A lamp that spits djinni that have gold coins...tell the others! Money's so scarce that no one can get it! How can one believe that it grows like that?"

"I'm telling the truth!" Catherine said, in a tone full of innocence. "And what I've told, I've seen—and as for Juliette, I don't know what Monsieur Bontems means."

"I know that before the Revolution," the Maire said, "that cottage had a chimney like that of a forge, and when I was there, by order of Monsieur le Curé, I saw diabolical things—but it could well be that someone was making false money there."

Grandvani's idea was seized with avidity, and immediately, Françoise was sent to fetch Juliette.

She came. Antoine was with her. They were holding hands, and the purest happiness animated their eyes, their movements and their expressions. They did not say a single word without consulting one another with their eyes, nor let a minute pass without looking at one another, and seemed to dread that Time, with all its centuries, would not have space enough to suffice for their tenderness. Antoine, tall and strong, and Juliette, thin, slender and pretty, were there before the Maire like a model, an eternal image, of a happy union.

"Let's see," said the Maire, "one of the gold coins of your dowry."

Juliette threw one on to the table and everyone made it resound on the tiles, on the mantelpiece, and it always sounded pure and agreeable: that harmonica, the sound of which brings down the consciences of men and the walls of cities, after which everyone runs, and the noisiest racket of which is not worth as much as one minute of pleasure.

"That's quite extraordinary!" exclaimed Grandvani, convinced that the coin was authentic.

"Well," said the farmer, already fearing that the thirty thousand francs might escape him, "since Mademoiselle Catherine is a witness to the fact, Antoine shall marry Juliette, provided that the existence if the lamp is verified. It will be good for the village if people can have everything they desire."

There was no talk of anything but the Marvelous Lamp throughout the village, and everyone's gaze was turned desirously toward the cottage. Some cast doubt on such an adventure; others, seeing Juliette and her dowry, wished that something similar might happen to them; in sum, everyone wanted to see the handsome inhabitant of the Devil's cottage.

In the midst of all these circumstances, there was such contentment at the fortunate success of Juliette and Antoine that every morning, the young women of the village came to put a flower on the banns attached to the door of the Mairie. Those ribbons and flowers, Catherine saw, and every day they excited a sharp pain in the depths of her heart, for Juliette's felicity made her compare her fate with her own, and that comparison was very cruel for her.

A few days after that scene she went to find Juliette and said to her: "You're lucky! Oh, my dear friend, I've inherited all your misfortune. I love your benefactor. Help me, I beg you, to remain alone in possession of going to the cottage on the hill. You can see that everyone in the village is talking about going to his dwelling to see him, and *it*, his lamp—for it's his lamp more than him that they want to examine. They'll importune him; he'll see other people than me. Isn't it enough that I already have his fay for a rival? Help me, then, my dear Juliette, and let's tell everyone that he has said that he only wants to communicate with one of us two, and you must take care, if anyone desires anything, always to leave it to me."

On hearing this speech, intermingled with tears, Juliette agreed to everything, but for her part she begged Catherine to make sure that the handsome stranger would come to her wedding and witness the happiness that was his work.

When news of that singular determination on the part of the chemist's son spread through the village, Jacques Bontemps, reflecting on the change in Catherine's behavior, began to suspect some "drollery," to use his expression, and he promised himself to discover the secret of the mysterious adventure.

Chapter XI
The Lamp is Stolen

One morning, Catherine returned to the cottage that contained all her life and happiness. She perceived Abel sitting on his bench, and from the moment that she saw the man she loved, her face lost the expression of meek melancholy that resided there, to take on that of the purest joy. But she saw immediately that Abel was sad, and immediately, she became sad, for she resembled those clouds in the sky that borrow their color from the sun.

"What's the matter?" she asked him, in a tone of voice that respired a tender compassion.

"Alas," he replied, "for three days I haven't seen my little fay; I can't live without seeing her. Oh, my dear Catherine, she infused me with life by a glance; far from her, or without her, everything is cold, colorless, dull, dead; nothing pleases me. Just now, I said something harsh to Caliban, and the poor man wept. I would have liked to put myself on my knees and beg his pardon, but when I saw my dolor, he claimed would like always to be maltreated thus. I wept in my turn, and I took refuge here, on this bench, in order to think about the pretty Pearl Fay."

"Is she very pretty, then?" asked Catherine, forgetting momentarily all the recommendations of the village.

"I don't really know," Abel replied, "for when I see her, I believe that I'm having a celestial vision that presents to me a pure soul, detached from all human circumstance."

"You don't love anyone in the world except her…?" asked Catherine, trembling.

"Yes," said Abel, "although I love no one but her amorously, for I sense that I love you."

Catherine remained pensive; that statement, although stripped of the sentiment that she wanted, nevertheless appeared to her to be a divine discourse.

Finally, she broke the silence in order to ask Abel to come to Juliette's wedding. Abel refused for a long time, but Catherine put so much charm and grace into her ardent persistence that the chemist's son agreed to come down to the village.

"Catherine," he said then, "that's on one condition. I haven't given you anything to remind you with what brotherly love I love you. I want you, at that fête where everyone will adorn themselves, to be brilliant. Will you come with me?"

And, taking her by the hand, he took her to the stone. Abel performed the usual ceremony there with the lamp, which he always carried on his person. The lovely djinni with the head crowned with flowers, always fresh and always new, appeared immediately, and Abel asked for a superb adornment for Catherine. The djinni plucked a long blade of grass still charged with dew, took the measurement of the blushing young woman's slender waist, and then promised to obey his master's order as promptly as possible.

Poor Catherine, full of joy—for she still had hope—announced the news to Juliette.

"He'll come," she said. "Undoubtedly, all gazes will fall upon him, but I alone will be able to press his hand, sense his soul. Oh, that happiness is a great deal; it's everything…yes, it's everything that I could ask of heaven!"

A few days later, Catherine was getting ready to go to bed. Suddenly, there is a loud noise in the square. She opens the window, and perceives a cavalier heading for the house. The cavalier draws nearer, and stops outside the door. Catherine goes downstairs, and, without saying a word, the stranger hands her a package on which she reads by the light of the moon, the only street-light there is in the village, which never runs out of gas: *To Mademoiselle Catherine Grandvani.*

As one can imagine, Catherine could hardly sleep when, after returning to her modest room, she unwrapped the parcel and admired a charming costume, consisting of a white satin under-dress and another dress that seemed to her to be lace but which, really, was actually a beautiful embroidered tulle. A row of false pearls, which she took for real daughters of the Oriental waves, played and ran through the sinuosities of the creases that formed its decoration, and the neckline of the charming dress had a grace that delighted Catherine. In fact, the top of the sleeves was garnished with seed-pearls, which played around the arms and the corsage, between her two lovely breasts, designing an inverted delta, which was terminated at each angle by masses of pearls.

A golden comb garnished with pearls, black satin shoes, and very fine glazed white gloves completed the outfit, but what showed that a woman had presided over that costume was that Catherine found at the bottom of the box a delightful necklace and earrings formed by large pieces of magnificent jet. Apparently, the fay had thought that she was the only one whose skin was so white that pearls could be confounded with it.

Was the black necklace an epigram addressed to her rival or a delicate attention? The question is difficult to decide, but at any rate, the necklace was the only thing that Catherine dared to try on. She took off her pretty collar, put the black necklace on, and jumped for joy, clapping her hands on seeing how her alabaster skin seemed a thousand times whiter by virtue of the effect of that jewelry.

She went to her casement, and looked into the air in the direction of the hill, and there, her heart addressed a thousand loving affections to her cherished idol; and she charged the zephyrs with her prayers; certainly, they had to fly less rapidly, and that night, the flowers did not curb their heads under the embalmed breath of the sons of Flora.

"It's true what they say," she added, on returning to her mirror. "A girl looks quite different with jewels! They give one an air..." And the poor child, intoxicated by a very forgivable pride—for it did not cause the loss of anyone—thinking of all brilliance with which she would shine at Juliette's wedding, ran to wake Francoise, and for a second time she ecstasized over her adornment, enjoying it doubly on seeing the maid's astonishment.

"Oh," she exclaimed, when she was in bed, "the man who gives such an adornment must love me..."

The day of Antoine and Juliette's wedding, so much desired, arrived. It would require the brush of the Dutch school to give an idea of the scene that the square in front of the church presented.

Fine sand had been strewn under the tufted elms, and formed a square area, at the end of which a few empty barrels, covered with planks, served as a throne for the two village fiddlers, whose violins were garnished with multicolored ribbons. Before that musical Areopagus, a crowd of young men and women, all dressed up, their faces imprinted with the frank gaiety born of the forgetfulness of labor, were laughing, dancing and frolicking with a sincerity, a noise and a confusion that inspired the desire to join in.

Around the square there were tables set up, and the old men in their best clothes were talking, arguing and rambling while serving themselves drinks or playing cards. A few, however, remained standing, hands behind their backs, contemplating the frolics of youth, remembering the years of their youth and making reflections on the approach of their winter. Those tanned faces, on which the words *fatigue* and *toil* were legible, were all smiling, and the songs of joy went as high as they could in the air. I imagine that there was some angel in heaven who, from the vault, was pouring down on them that spirit of the forgetfulness of evils, the most precious gift of all.

The fortunate couple had not yet arrived, and Catherine was also missing. After mass, Catherine had got dressed furtively, and had gone furtively to fetch her dear Abel. So, after the dance, people looked toward the street, and a grave anxiety was manifest on the faces of the wedding guests, deprived of the sovereigns of the celebration. An even more powerful curiosity agitated minds, for it had not been forgotten that Juliette had boasted of seeing at her wedding her handsome benefactor, the chemist's son.

"Will he come with his lamp?" asked a young peasant-woman.

"It's said that he's as handsome as an angel," said another.

"Do you know," said a farmer to one of his colleagues, in a corner, "that fat Mathurin isn't sure of renewing his lease for the beautiful farm of Madame la

Duchesse de Sommerset,[13] the rich English princess, and that there's a good thing to be obtained by offering twelve thousand francs for it. If this lamp of which there's so much talk has the power to sign leases, that would be even better."

"Do you believe these stupid things?" replied the farmer.

At that moment, little children appeared in the high street of the village, running with an air of astonishment that gave rise to the belief that something extraordinary was happening. They turned their heads repeatedly, stopped, looked, and then ran on in silence, as if stupefied.

Soon, Catherine was seen arriving in the square, in her brilliant outfit, giving her arm to Antoine, and the chemist's son was conducting the lovely Juliette. Antoine's father was following Abel respectfully, for a man who throws thirty thousand francs to a young woman as one throws a piece of bread to a stray dog, is not to be disdained.

At the sight of that quadrille, silence fell, and people formed a hedge as they passed by; it seemed that no one had enough eyes to contemplated Abel, whose singular costume and striking beauty astonished all the peasants. The lamp especially, the lamp that he wore

---

[13] When the author improvised this title, he might not have known that there was an actual Duchess of Somerset (with one m) in the early 1820s: the former Lady Charlotte Douglas-Hamilton, who had married the eleventh Duke, Edward Adolphus St. Maur, a noted mathematician. Although Balzac's fictitious duchess is English, I have retained the French form of her title, in order to emphasize her distinction from the actual duchess.

suspended around his neck, as the most precious thing in the world, since it came from the Pearl Fay, seemed a sun of which everyone wanted to have a ray. It was not until that first furor of curiosity had been slaked that a long murmur was heard when people saw Catherine so beautiful and so resplendent.

The tax-collector found himself beside Jacques Bontems, who, at the sight of Catherine dressed so sumptuously, frowned and moved his head in a singular manner. The tax-collector said to one of his partisans, loudly enough for the cuirassier to hear: "That's what comes from knowing enchanters! They give beautiful dresses; look at Mademoiselle Catherine; she's rubbed the lamp nicely, for it's said that it's necessary to rub it to have what one wants."

The ironic tone of these words inflamed the sergeant, who turned to the tax-collector and looked at him in a fashion to make him fall silent immediately.

"Bag of numbers," he exclaimed, "by my *bancal*"—that is what cuirassiers call their sabers—"he hasn't got anything that I don't...if I ever hear another syllable of slander against Catherine, I'll cut off the orator's ears, you hear...march in step, and beware bombs!"

Jacques Bontems loved Catherine, and he loved her profoundly, although his abrupt manners and his exterior seemed incompatible with such a delicate sentiment. The cuirassier's sentiment was like the canvas of a great painter depicting a violently agitated man: you look, and nothing betrays the emotion; you examine closely, and the manner in which he is holding his hand, his foot or in which he sticks out his chest gives you a cold sweat; thus, a single word or gesture on Jacques' part said everything: he would die for Catherine, with the same sang-froid with which he would have obeyed his captain.

Abel was standing by the barrels; it goes without saying that Catherine was not elsewhere. Jacques came to find the Maire's daughter, and looked at her with an expression of interest and dolor. He whispered in her ear, in such a manner that no one else could hear:

"Catherine, I love you to the utmost depths of my heart, and if you were smitten with another, I wouldn't love you any less, but my child, vanity will doom you; these beautiful clothes betray you, and everyone is talking about it. You can be more beautiful for the others, but for those who love you, under whatever form they see you, you'll be the same. Who gave you that outfit?"

"The lamp," she said blushing.

"The lamp!" repeated the cuirassier, shaking his head. "Oh, Catherine, Catherine, I'll make sure of that...!"

The pretty girl did not hear the last words. In fact, the presence of Abel, who only talked to her, and who remained by her side, had rendered Catherine drunk with happiness. She was cheerful, lively and animated, and her amorous folly seemed to spread through the whole assembly.

At every moment Catherine wanted to collect Abel's words, interrogate his soul, keep a lookout for his gazes, play with the lamp that a silk cord passed around his neck suspended over his heart; and Abel, for his part, with the naivety that distinguished him, passed his fingers through Catherine's hair and held her hand in front of everyone—and everyone envied Catherine's happiness, and no one, even Grandvani, dared to speak to the young man, who, by his pose and his expression, resembled a rock rising in the sea, at the base of which the inhabitants of the bitter waters were playing.

"You're very pretty today, Catherine," Abel said to her, and Catherine, while dancing, smiling at everyone, said to Juliette: "I'm the happiest person there is on earth at this moment; he will love me, and the fervor of my love will be his recompense."

There had never been a happier day for Catherine, an epoch of her life more beautiful and more gracious; and the simplest incidents were for her events that were engraved in her memory in an ineradicable fashion.

While she was dancing with an abandon, a charm and a celestial pleasure, her black necklace came undone, and fell to the ground at Abel's feet. He picked it up, and held it in his hands or a long time, crumpling it, playing with it, turning it around.

After the quadrille, Catherine noticed the absence of her necklace, and looked for it. Abel, who was hiding it in his bosom, left her prey to her anxiety for a few moments.

"My necklace!" she said—and everyone looked for it.

"I only attach value to it," she said to Abel, "because it comes from you!"

Abel took it out of his bosom, kissed the necklace, and put it around Catherine's neck himself. Furtively, she kissed the necklace in the same place. From that day on, the necklace was her entire treasure.

After each quadrille she ran to Abel with the joy, the lightness and the happiness of a young fawn returning to its mother after playing momentarily in the fresh grass. To gaze at that cherished lover while she danced, to desire the end of the figure in order to find herself at his side and hold his hand: such were the trivia that nuanced her happiness and her evening with accidents of pain and pleasure.

It is necessary to have loved, necessary to have felt one's breast torn by the last stroke of the hour of the rendezvous, when one has said: "At that hour, I'll be waiting for you," to understand Catherine's joy, and to feel her pure voluptuousness on the reading this account of the simple events that form great gifts for the heart.

Catherine felt such a benevolence in her soul that she ran at times to Jacques Bontems' side, teased him, laughed with him—and the poor cuirassier was content with that reflected happiness, so much grace and gentility did Catherine put into it. In sum, she appeared so charming that all the young women and young men, the women and the old men—the entire village—admired her and looked at her, not with envy, but the sentiment that is suspended between admiration and jealousy.

That fête was her triumph, the most beautiful day of her life, and all that celestial brightness came from the presence of the man she loved; she was unconscious of the future, and enjoyed the present that she was embracing with ardor.

In the middle of the celebration someone brought the sergeant a package stamped with the seal of the Ministry of Finance. Catherine was next to Jacques when the man who had gone to collect the letters brought that important dispatch.

"Ah!" said Catherine. "You're always telling us about your correspondence with Ministers—I want to know how they talk and write. Give me that, Jacques."

"No, Catherine, no," the cuirassier replied, seeing that the tax-collector was coming, fearing that the document might announce the appointment of his rival.

"When one loves someone," Catherine replied, "one does not hide anything from them..." And the impertinent young woman ran to Abel's side, holding the package and making as if to open it.

"Well, swear that you'll marry me if that letter contains my appointment, or if it gives me the hope of being appointed."

"Marry!" repeated Catherine, looking in turn at the cuirassier, the letter and Abel. Everyone formed a circle around them and waited impatiently.

Jacques was not tranquil, for they were about to discover the truth regarding his pretended credit, and Catherine was holding his fate in her hands.

Catherine, looking at the lamp, judged that she was not promising anything much, for she said to herself: *The djinni, being all-powerful, will disengage me from my promise if Abel comes to love me.* She promised before all the village to marry the cuirassier if the letter gave him the hope of being tax-collector, and Père Grandvani pledged his word with that of his daughter.

The cuirassier changed color when he saw the envelope fall, and silence reigned.

Abel watched the scene curiously, without understanding any of it. During the entire fête he had had the insouciance that melancholy gives, and he had not thought about anything except his fay; he was there without being there.

Scarcely had Catherine read the first lines than she folded up the letter and handed it back to Jacques Bontems, who believed, with the entire village, that Catherine would become his wife.

The tax-collector frowned, but had reason to be joyful, because Bontems' face did not announce pleasure. In fact, this is what the letter contained:

Monsieur,

His Excellency was indignant at the fashion in which you have requested his protection, and only the memory of the obligation that Monseigneur has to you has preserved you from the effects of his anger. Calumny, when one has been a soldier, is a poor means of reaching one's goal; the employee whose dismissal you seek is an honest man, and has always fulfilled his duties well; he has not yet acquired the length of service necessary for his retirement, and the style of your petition has not engaged His Excellency to find other employment for you.

Etc.

Devastated, Jacques Bontems admired Catherine's delicacy, but when Grandvani came to him to ask what news he had received, he had no other resource but to summon all his audacity, and replied that he would be appointed to the position of tax-collector, and that His Excellency had just promised it to him, as soon as another position could be found for the present tax-collector.

"Well, that won't take long, Monsieur Bontems," replied the tax-collector. "The postmaster of L*** has just died; if I'm given that post, I'll gladly cede this one to you..."

"We'll see!" replied Bontems, with the air of a minister in favor. "We'll see...in due time."

The pensive cuirassier contemplated Abel and Catherine, and quivered with rage. Suddenly, on seeing the ribbon that held the marvelous Lamp, he conceived the idea of rendering himself master of it. *If that lamp,* he said to himself, *has given thirty thousand francs, dresses and jewels, if it's as powerful as people say, the djinni that I'll have at my orders will get me the position.*

So, when the fête was on the point of ending, when night had fallen and Abel talked about going home, Jacques Bontems slipped behind the barrels, equipped himself with a pair of scissors, cut the ribbon, seized the precious talisman, and, before Abel had perceived it, was already far away, the possessor of the miraculous jewel and prey to the most vivid joy.

Juliette and Catherine escorted Abel back to the cottage. Caliban was waiting for him impatiently. When he separated from the two young women he embraced them with an entirely virginal candor, and Catherine went back to her modest room, fell to her knees and sent a fervent prayer of thanks to heaven for the happiness of that day; Abel's kiss, chaste as it was, was still burning her lips.

Chapter XII
Abel in the Empire of the Fays

The wily cuirassier could not contain the joy of having the lamp. He took one of his former comrades into his confidence, and for half the night they were with regard to the talisman like La Fontaine's shoemaker with his hundred écus; they did not know where to put it. The cuirassier, ignorant of the formalities that it was necessary to fulfill in order to make the djinni of the lamp appear, had rubbed and appealed, but nothing came. They were forced to wait for daylight, and Jacques Bontems promised himself to learn from Catherine the manner in which one made use of the talisman.

The soldier therefore went to see Catherine, and after a thousand detours, he got round to asking for information about the chemist's son, pretending to refuse to believe in the power of the lamp. He made Catherine spell out everything that was done to evoke the djinni. Then, at nightfall, the sergeant went to the hill with his comrade, and after having searched for and found the stone, they made the little djinni appear, who sang them the song of obedience.

The cuirassier and the hussar stood there open-mouthed in admiration before the group that was offered to their eyes: the beauty of the pretty girl who was looking at them with surprise, while bowing before the lamp, caused them to forget what they wanted.

"I'd gladly give that implement," said the hussar, "to marry that little djinni."

"What do you wish?" repeated the pretty soft voice.

"I want you," said the cuirassier, "to obtain immediately for Jacques Bontems, former sergeant of the cuirassiers of the guard, the post of tax-collector of the
commune of V***, and, if possible, the post of postmaster of L*** for the man who is the present tax-collector,
for it's necessary not to injure anyone's interests."

The negro and the djinni looked at one another. The
African disappeared and came back promptly to write,
under Jacques' dictation, what he wanted. When that
was done, the djinni cried, waving the golden scarf:

"Before your eyes have tasted sleep three times,
breathed six thousand times and seen three dawns and
three evening dews, you will have been satisfied. I shall
race through the air, traverse the skies, and my master
will be content."

A blue-tinted flame escaped from beneath their
throne, and they disappeared, leaving the two soldiers
prey to the strangest surprise.

"Jacques," said the hussar, "it's not good to have
only thought of yourself; could you not have asked for
something for me? I could marry Antoine's sister if I had
money. The Duchesse de Sommerset's farm is up for
lease—ask for the lease for me. Fat Thomas wants to
give fifteen thousand francs, try to get the Duchess to
cede it to me for twelve thousand; I'll marry Antoine's
sister, and I'll become rich.

Jacques rubbed the lamp, and summoned the djinni,
which appeared with the same submission.

"Go find the Duchesse de Sommerset," he said to
her. "Make her lease her farm to Jean Leblanc, former
hussar of the guard, for twelve thousand francs, and
bring the lease to be signed as soon as possible, with
fifty bottles of champagne that we'll drink in honor of
the duchesse, the prettiest woman in the world. And I

also want the lawsuit that is troubling the Maire of the commune so much to be terminated. Go."

"Before you have bought what is necessary to exploit the farm Des Granges, you shall have the least duly signed," said the djinni, and disappeared.

"It's a true miracle!" exclaimed the cuirassier. "Provided that we're not being led a dance."

They tried to lift the stone, making every effort to discover, in the moonlight, the mechanism that fitted it to the ground; they could not do it, and they went away making a thousand plans, the cuirassier for the time when he would be the tax-collector and Catherine's husband, the hussar for when he would be a farmer and Suzette's husband.

They went away singing with joy, the new tax-collector already sending out his notifications, and the farmer counting his cattle and sheep.

While they were building their castles in Spain, Abel was plunged into the greatest chagrin. He had lost is dear lamp; he had searched everywhere and had not found it. Aided by Caliban, he set out for the village, suspecting that they might find it on the way if it had fallen, and expecting—the good souls!—that if someone had picked it up, they would return it. Never had the plaints of a lover who has lost his mistress or a child his mother approached the dolor that burst forth in Abel's regrets.

Half way down, they met the lovely Catherine, whose pure and light voice was murmuring a love song.

"What's wrong, my Abel?" she said, fearfully, stopping and taking his hand. "You're sad—oh, tell me why you're suffering! Tears that one sheds together are not bitter, and I sense that I would be happy if you spread pain in my heart."

"Catherine," he said, "I've lost my lamp..."

At that point, the Maire's daughter stopped him; she was utterly nonplussed, and the state of her soul can only be compared to that of a dark room into which a ray of sunlight had been introduced. In fact, Jacques' curious interrogations came to mind like a flash of light.

"Abel," she said, "it's me who is the cause of your trouble, because it was at my plea that you came down to the village; it's up to me to do everything possible to recover the lamp that has been stolen from you. Wait for me, hope, and you'll see me again shortly."

She leapt through the brambles and thorn-bushes, and, taking the shortest and most difficult route, she was reminiscent of a bird skimming the hill, and felt a thousand times lighter in running for her dear Abel.

Caliban watched her, fearing that she might fall down at any moment, but a God sustained her: the lively, light, mutinous God of infancy, the God of life.

She traverses the meadow, arrives in the village and runs to Bontems' house, opens the door violently and falls into his cottage like a bomb. She sees the cuirassier and his comrade in contemplation before the lamp.

Before Jacques has made a movement, she has seized it and, launching a thunderous glare at Jacques, says to him: "How have you been able to deprive Juliette's benefactor of his talisman? It will be the death of the poor child!"

Jacques and Jean are stupefied. Catherine escapes, and runs with even more ardor toward the fill. The people of the village who see her flying thus with the lamp, think that the magical talisman is enabling her to walk on air, and someone goes to tell Grandvani that his daughter, astride the lamp, has been borne away who knows where...

She arrives breathless, and shouts to Abel from the bottom of the hill: "Abel, Abel, here it is! Don't worry..."

She climbs the mountain, reaches him, gives him the lamp, and he yields to joy on seeing that present from his little fay.

"Abel," she said, emotionally, "Catherine can die if, once in her life, she has been able to cause you a moment of pleasure..."

"Pleasure…," said Abel. "That word isn't strong enough..."

"I can die, then," she replied, confounding her soul with Abel's with her gaze. "I can die, Abel!"

"Is it not my fay who gave it to me?" he said, kissing his lamp.

"That remark caused Catherine to become as still as a marble statue. That remark had resounded in her diaphragm, striking her like a dagger-thrust.

"Abel, she said, finally, "permit your little Catherine to ask one thing of you..." She stopped, looked at him dolorously, and then continued: "I'd like you to promise me to do what I desire without knowing yet what it is."

"I promise," he said.

"Well," the pretty peasant girl continued, "I'd like to see the fay without being seen by her. I want to know whether she's so pretty, so very pretty, that nothing in the world can efface her..."

"I'll try," said Abel. "One night, you can try to hide in the laboratory."

"She loves you very much, then, that fay?"

"I'm content to love her," Abel replied, "and I dare not hope that she has any love for me..."

"You'd be happy, then," Catherine continued, "cherishing a supernatural being who doesn't love you!"

Abel said nothing. That silence was equivalent to hope for the poor peasant girl, who after having contemplated her beloved, went slowly back to her house, sat down beside her father, told him about the theft of the lamp, and, dreaming and sighing, felt tears brimming in her eyes a thousand times over during the day, gazing at the wall, and thinking that she could see Abel.

A few days later, a courier traversed the village rapidly, stopped at Jacques Bontems' door, handed him a packet bearing the seal of the Minister of Finance, and the cuirassier, when he opened it, found his appointment to the position of tax-collector, that of the tax-collector to the position of postmaster, a royal edict terminating the lawsuit, and a promise of a lease signed by the Duchesse de Sommerset, just as Jacques Bontems had wished; and, in a letter, a notary indicated that Jean Leblanc was awaited any day to sign the document."

"What about the bottles of champagne?" Jacques asked.

"They've been in your cellar for some time," replied the messenger, who remounted his horse and disappeared at a fast gallop.

The stupefied cuirassier went down into his cellar, and did indeed find the bottles carefully laid out on laths, so well arranged that he could not doubt that it had not been done recently. Then he was at the peak of his joy. He went triumphantly to Grandvani's house, followed by the tax-collector and Jean Leblanc, handed the Maire the king's edict, and requested Catherine's hand.

At that request, the poor child went pale, blush, trembled, and could not find any other expedient, for the moment, than to ask for a brief delay, which was accorded to her.

Let us leave Jean Leblanc and Jacques Bontems regretting that they had not asked the djinni of the lamp for an income of a hundred thousand livres, Catherine weeping, and the village prey to surprise and admiration, regretting that the curé was absent, in order that they might discover whether one was committing a sin in believing in the omnipotence of fays, and let us return to the chemist's cottage, his son and the charming Pearl Fay.

For several days, Abel had been deprived of the divine apparitions of the tender genius that he adored. His melancholy was beginning to become extreme, and Caliban was already anxious in seeing his master's cheeks pale and a kind of folly presiding over his thoughts and movements.

"I can't live without her," he said to the old servant. "Everything is insupportable to me; I'm experiencing difficulty living, and if life is a feast, I'm not hungry, my poor Caliban."

One night, he was profoundly asleep; he sensed himself, in his slumber, being rapidly drawn away; it seemed to him that he had wings and that he was flying; he put out his hands in front of him, thinking that he might spare himself a fall, and he woke up at that painful moment...

He was beside her, in an airborne chariot; she was watching him sleep, and when he woke up, his gaze still embarrassed by the swathes of slumber, was confounded in the sparkling eyes of the Pearl Fay. The infernal horses were drawing them like a cloud driven by a tempestuous wind.

Abel was almost in the fay's arms; he could savor her breath, and he was afraid of having profaned her breast, for he had the vague thought that his head had rested upon that throne of amour.

She was still looking at him without saying a word, and her eyes seemed to be emitting a moist flame, on which Abel nourished himself avidly.

"Where am I?" he asked, finally.

"Next to your fay," she replied, in a celestial voice, which made Abel's heart beat faster.

"Where are we going?"

"To the Empire of the Fays. Haven't you desired to witness the magical scenes in which djinni, enchanters and fays are present? My chariot is taking you to one of their most brilliant assemblies."

"What!" he exclaimed. "I'm going to see them face to face?"

"Yes, the fay replied, "but on one condition, which is that when I tell you to, you close your eyes, for you'd risk losing your sight if the light struck you at certain moments."

Abel promised what the fay had asked of him with as simple nod of the head, for he was plunged in a divine admiration in contemplating the rare beauty of the Pearl Fay. She was dressed with a sumptuous elegance, which doubled her charms, without that glamour harming the tenderness of her character, which was painted on her pretty face in love and generosity.

Her head was crowned with flowers and fruits, artistically placed, the black curls of her hair hanging over her forehead and coming to play near her eyes, in such a fashion as to further increase the delicacy of her gaze and double the gleam of her satined skin and its vivid colors.

She fell silent, but her gaze, alternately aimed at Abel and immediately lowered, seemed to speak, and told Abel to speak in his turn, and that, whatever discourse emerged from his mouth, it would be welcomed with gratitude. Their thoughts, during that charming silence, were doubtless voyaging in the same region, for their hands came together, squeezing ne another involuntarily, and Abel cried, with gracious naivety:

"I'm suffering! My heart is swelling!"

"Are you in pain?" asked the fay.

"No," he said. "I think, on the contrary, that it's too much happiness..."

The fay blushed, and turned her eyes away; she made no reply, and that moment never left Abel's memory. He felt then sufficient boldness to speak about his amour, but an invincible dread, a modesty of sentiment, froze his senses and held his tongue captive.

Throughout the time the journey lasted, only their eyes spoke, and a charming smile often came to wander on their lips, and made them both comprehend that they understood one another. Does anyone know anything more delightful than that language of the soul, that sympathetic force, which, without the incomplete assistance of human speech, causes you to sense what the cherished object that you love thinks and desires?

In that pure region of thought, disengaged from the gross sensations of the body, a subtle charm reigns that no human speech can render, since no human thought can give the idea of a mystery that has to be felt by the soul; it seems that in those exceedingly rare moments, a light flame wings its way from one heart to the other, bearing light and thought successively, and a freshness, an indescribable delight; perhaps that is the way that angels communicate in heaven.

Once two individuals have mingled their sentiments in that fashion, and their perfect accord has rendered a similar note, having, so to speak, sung the same hymn, it is impossible for them to conceive of a separation, or an absence; they love one another, and always, even at a distance of a thousand leagues, their souls will have similar movements.

Abel and the Pearl Fay savored that superhuman voluptuousness, and those two marvels of nature, having souls worthy of the perfection of their bodies, understood one another perfectly and so well that by the end of the journey, Abel's eyes having become increasing expressive, the charming fay made a divine little gesture with her fan, full of delicacy and grace, as if to lower her beautiful long-lashed eyelids, and sais to him: "Silence, Abel—you talk too much!"

At that remark, the only one that had been pronounced for an hour, they looked at one another and started laughing.

"Oh," said Abel, "I know of nothing more delightful than an amour that grows in the midst of exquisite luxury and elegance. To see you always ornamented, respiring the sweetest perfumes, surrounded by the prestige of your power…it's too much…if I don't have your protection, I want to die."

"You, die? Oh, live, Abel, live to spread through the world the influence of your beautiful soul."

At that moment, she placed her hand over Abel's eyes, and Abel heard a noise and a confusion, a multitude of cries and voices; but after a quarter of an hour, it stopped. The fay instructed him to keep his eyes closed, and, taking him by the hand, she guided him through corridors and staircases. Finally, they reached a place where the little fay made Abel sit down, and permitted him to open his eyes, while only looking at her.

"Even if the heavens were open," he said, "I could only see you..."

As he finished, an intoxicating music commenced; and when the fay lowered with her pretty hand a panel that was in front of them, Abel remained mute with surprise before the magical scene that was offered to his gaze.

A vast circular space decorated with golden columns and garlands, rose-windows, nets, plinths and golden ornaments, contained an innumerable crowd of djinn and enchanters; the circus was black; from stage to stage Abel perceived a host of fays, each prettier than the rest. They appeared to be surrounded by a cloud of light, for between each row of fays there was a diamond chandelier covered with candles that spread a marvelous glow; their costumes competed in richness and elegance; they were laughing, chatting and joking with enchanters and djinn, who were mingled with them. An immense sun, brilliant and ornamented with crystals, sowed furrows of light, which seemed to sprinkle an entire dew of vivid and scintillating radiance within the superb palace.

The most profound silence fell, and everyone listened attentively to the divine music whose sounds spread out through the palace. Abel thought he was in heaven and listening to magical chords played by angels. He was profoundly moved, and could only squeeze the hand of his little fay, who enjoyed his astonishment with an indescribable pleasure.

"Hide yourself well in this corner," she told him, for if my companions the fays perceive the presence of a mortal by my side, I'm doomed! I've already had difficulty getting you through, although dressed as a djinni."

In fact, Abel was wearing a costume absolutely similar to the most beautiful garments that he saw on the djinn. He turned round and looked at himself in a mirror, admired that enchantment on seeing himself, and experienced a kind of surge of coquetry on perceiving that he was more handsome than the majority of the djinn he could see.

Suddenly, the music stopped, and a tap of the wand of the djinni who was conducting the music caused a magical decoration suddenly to rise up, which attracted Abel's attention, and an even more surprising spectacle plunged him into an ocean of new enjoyments.

A palace ornamented by a profusion of marble and porphyry columns, with galleries extending as far as the eye could see, an ornamentation of a miraculous sumptuousness, was offered to his gaze, as if by enchantment; a host of gracious fays and djinn, magnificently dressed, some of whom resembled the djinni of the lamp, intoned a song of joy, which confused his ears slightly; but the pretty Pearl Fay told him that it was because he was not a djinni, that the song was only appropriate to the immortal troop of enchanters, and that humans could not comprehend it.

"Wait a while," she continued, "And you'll see the djinn prey to a species of frenzy that will make them raise their hands and strike them against one another furiously; for things happen here that will surprise you."

Indeed, after a quarter of an hour, there was such a din that Abel was obliged to block his ears; meanwhile, a number of marvels succeeded one another to astonish him; for a palace, a forest, fields and cottages had been substituted; for the cottage, a enchanted garden; for the garden, a dungeon; for the dungeon, places that delighted him with admiration.

He had not enough eyes or ears, to hear the songs and the music and to see the voluptuous dances of the prettiest fays. Those magical tableaux were intermingled with piquant and spiritual remarks by the Pearl Fay, who, at intervals, explained to him the usages of the empire of the fays.

"The djinn you see assembled here," she told him, "have singular manias; one can touch their hand, the fingers, the arm, the shoulder—the entire body, in fact, except the cheek; as soon as a djinni's cheeks is even brushed by another djinni, it can only be washed away with blood; it's one of those bizarreries to which enchanters are subject.

"Then again, they have what they call their patriotism, which consists of praising themselves for their courage and glory; it would be a crime to recognize the courage of other nations of djinn.

"That's not all; you see those enchanters who are wearing something red on their vestment? Well, that ribbon is one of their passions. Suspend a delicacy in a room and bring dogs; they will wear themselves out leaping in order to seize a few morsels; it is the same for djinn and the ribbon; they wear themselves out and consume themselves in efforts to have a fragment, but once they have it, it is no longer of any consequence to them.

"Finally, you see the djinn in very white shirts with neat clothing and exquisite jewelry—that, alas, is what pleases them most. If you were not dressed as fastidiously as you are at this moment, Abel, for all your sensible, noble and proud soul, in spite of the cortege of virtues and graces that accompany you, with your beautiful face, the most rascally of enchanters would have preference over you, if he were well-dressed.

"Among other usages, there are djinn who preach the art of learning to die, and even if one does not succeed the first time, they continue to recommend it. Then too, if among the djinn there are striking individuals, so long as they are alive, no one takes any notice of them; as soon as they are dead, they are celebrated. In general, the djinn here put grandeur into petty things, and pettiness into great ones. It is necessary to spend ten times as much in order to stroll as to eat; there are even animals that cost more to maintain than humans.

"Finally, the religion of djinn consists of kneeling down, reading in a book and listening to hymns; but of doing good, helping the unfortunate, setting aside the self and forgetting it a little, oh, there are only very rare good djinn who combine one with the other—which is to say, the exterior religion with the interior religion that is seated in the conscience. For the most part, the exterior religion is everything, and they believe that heaven is won, as a game of chess is won, by dint of maneuvers."

"What you are telling me there," replied Abel, "astonishes me even more than what I see."

"Oh," she said, "you will learn many other things even more astonishing..."

After a thousand enchantments, each more extraordinary than the last, the pretty fay ordered her young protégé to close his eyes, and she transported him to her palace. There he had complete liberty to come and go. A pretty girl, one of the fay's slaves, took him to a place almost as lovely as the boudoir of pearls that he had seen before. He lay down in a bed whose sheets were dazzlingly white, and the following day, the fay came to wake him up with the sounds of an instrument that rendered an enchanting melody.

The Pearl Fay rejoiced in Abel's awakening, as nature does in the return of the sun. She was dressed with a simplicity that contrasted with her vestments of the day before. After asking her young protégé how he liked it in the empire of the fays, while sitting on his bed, and having frolicked with the child of nature, she left him in order to prepare for him, with her own hands, a meal entirely new to him.

Indeed, everything—the unfamiliar dishes, the precious crystal, the tablecloth, the silverware and the furniture—was a subject of astonishment for Abel.

The pretty fay served him and shared everything with him; a tender amour, pure and celestial, spread an indefinable magic over those two charming individuals. How could poor Catherine be anything to Abel, and enter into comparison with the Pearl Fay?

Catherine was in love, her heart knew all the love of nature; she had an admirable simplicity and candor; but the fairy had just as much love, which she testified in a less naïve but perhaps more gracious manner, and to simplicity she added all the majesty and seductions of wealth, and the cortege of fortune and power. Furthermore, she was loved—what am I saying?—adored! So Abel's amour, combined with hers, embellished every movement, every word, every smile, with a charm that Catherine certainly found in Abel, but which Abel did not find in Catherine.

Abel spent in the fay's palace moments of happiness that no discourse can render. Finally, one evening, he fell to his knees, and declared his passion to her, and no man ever spoke more eloquently than him.

The next day he woke up; the smile with which the fay had welcomed his speech was still so deeply engraved in his heart that he believed that he saw her, presented her with his hand, and furtively wiped away a tear. He looked around to admire the sumptuousness of the place where he slept; he saw the laboratory, his cottage, the retorts, and the dust.

The cricket was singing; that was the only music that greeted his awakening. He thought that he had been dreaming and had emerged too soon, alas, from enchanting illusions of a dream of amour.

Chapter XIII
What the Pearl Fay Is

Abel got dressed, and, seeing the garments of his dream, began to believe that the multiple sensations that he had experienced might have been real, even though they had been surrounded by the vaporous cloud that surrounds nocturnal illusions. He saw Caliban coming toward him; the worthy old servant rejoiced in seeing his master again, and son drew him outside the cottage. He showed him poor Catherine sitting on the stone. The pretty peasant girl was posed with grace, but the sharpest dolor was painted in her attitude.

Abel took a few steps; she raised her head, uttered a cry, and threw herself, weeping, into the young man's arms.

"For three days," she said, "I've come every morning, waiting for my daylight, my sun...but nothing dissipated the night of my soul. I said to myself every time, as I climbed the hill: 'Today he'll be there!' I said it to myself, and when I went down again I was sad, because you hadn't arrived. Oh, if I had an enemy, and I wished him harm, I would like him to wait for three days...for someone he loved."

"Catherine! My dear Catherine!"

Oh, dear Abel, how handsome you are! Oh, let me look at you..."

"It's the fay who wove this fine linen, it's her who embroidered the flowers on that precious fabric..."

The fay...always the fay...

"Oh, Catherine, she loves me…I'm certain of it…I've seen her palace, the empire of the fays...I'm dazed by it."

And Abel told Catherine about the marvels that he had witnessed, and the delicate attentions of the fay: how she had poured the milk to temper a divine liquid that spread the activity of thought through the mind, and animated amour, etc., etc.

"I would do it as well as her," said Catherine, with a sulky expression. "Abel, I implore you, let me witness an apparition of the fay."

"Come this evening," Abel replied to her. "She ought to come to take back the lamp, of which she says I have no more need—for, Catherine, I dare not tell you my hope."

"She'll marry you! The fay!"

"I believe so," he replied. "But I don't know how a man can become the husband of a fay…"

"Can one be happy," Catherine replied, "married to a woman who has more power than us? If she deceived you…"

"Impossible" cried Abel. "Impossible! To say that, it's necessary not to have seen her smile."

Catherine looked at Abel, savored that sight, so desired, and could not help bursting into tears. She fled, after having promised to come back that evening.

She did in fact, come at nightfall; she had helped to put her aged father to bed, who had scolded her softly because, he said, at the approach of her marriage, she was running around too much, alone and in the fields; Jacques Bontems had complained about it.

She had calmed her father down with caresses and kisses. Then, taking Françoise into her confidence, she quit her virginal bed in order to run to the cottage to see her beloved again.

He was sitting in the worm-eaten armchair that had been the delight of his infancy, with his elbows on the table where Caliban had once cleaned the grain, and he was thinking about his fay. The antique lamp illuminated the laboratory. Catherine made a sign to Caliban, slid lightly through the partly-open door, and, approaching Abel very quietly, greeted him with a kiss.

"Oh! It's you, Catherine?"

"Yes," she said. "I've come to see the fay."

"Where shall we hide you?" he replied, looking around.

Caliban's advice prevailed, and it was decided that he large worm-eaten armchair would be placed between the oven and the fireplace, and that, in the small space that was found there, Catherine would crouch down silently, and as soon as the fay stirred she would lower her head and make herself as small as possible.

Catherine, genteel and cheerful, chatted to Abel all evening, and the gentle manners of the chemist's son gave her hope every time she conversed and played with him.

Finally, Abel lay down on his bed. Caliban withdrew, and on the stroke of midnight, a soft music announced the apparition of the Pearl Fay. She came in her brilliant costume, more beautiful, daintier and more vivacious than ever. She wandered around the laboratory, touched with her hands everything of which Abel made use, talked to him, and listened to him.

They sat on the bed, and there, the pretty fay, deploying her graces and the prestige of her coquetry, appeared to Catherine to be the queen of nature. The peasant girl, hidden in her corner, put her handkerchief over her mouth, so that in the silence, no one would hear her sighs and sobs, for she despaired of ever prevailing over a creature as astonishing as the Pearl Fay.

Alas, she said to herself, *why has the sun, in spite of all my precautions, adulterated the whiteness of my hands? Why am I not a fay? Oh, yes, she's a fay, for there's no woman on earth who can have that intelligence, that grace! Great God! Amour is lodged in her eyes. What a gaze!*

"Abel," said the fay, "in a little while you shall know to what I'm submitting myself in order to make our happiness. You won't see me again except as a mortal; I'm abdicating my empire for you..."

What proof of love more beautiful than that can I give him? Catherine said to herself, and wept, dampening the handkerchief she was holding with tears.

Abel, at the peak of joy, ardently kissed the fay's hands; he covered her with kisses; she smiled secretly—which broke Catherine's heart—and finally, she deposited a farewell kiss on Abel's lips, which left the chemist's son like a marble statue. A divine fire was flowing through his veins instead of blood, and he felt his heart falter; he fell on to his bed.

The fay disappeared then, taking the marvelous lamp with her.

Abel was recalled to life by the gentle Catherine; she was weeping hot tears, and her chagrin was so violent that Abel despaired of knowing what to do to soothe Catherine's dolor.

"She's too beautiful! Oh, yes, you have to love her, you can't do otherwise, and I...I have nothing more to do than die; I want to kill myself. Where are the poisons? Kill me, Abel. I feel that I can't live without

156

you…you're more to me than a brother…oh, what will I become?"

Abel spent the rest of the night soothing Catherine; He could only calm her despair by abusing her and swearing to her that he loved her tenderly, that they would always be together. Catherine replied that she knew full well that he was deceiving her by speaking to her thus, but that she loved him even more for hearing him say it; and, lulled by a hope of which she knew the scant reality, she dried her tears and became tranquil again.

That scene can only be compared to those with which the infancy of all humans has been sown: the dolor of a child who wants the impossible, which has been refused to him, and to whom one ends up promising the moon whose crescent he sees in the water, once it is full; that naïve infantile dolor, deceived by a gross ruse, is the image of the scene of chagrin to which Catherine rendered the smoky laboratory witness.

In the morning, she began reasoning again; she recovered courage, embraced Abel and quit his dwelling, resolved never to return.

On leaving the cottage, she was so troubled by her somber despair, and by the idea that it was necessary to marry Jacques Bontems, that she took the path to the forest. She looked at the ground as she went, drying up many a tear.

Suddenly, she noticed pearls on the path, which announced that the fay had passed that way. On closer inspection she saw on the sand the marks of carriage wheels, and their small breadth indicated an elegant vehicle. She decided to follow the route that the fay's rig had taken, and as she followed that route, ever step she took slid a ray of hope into her soul.

She walked for a long time, and when she was three-quarters of the way through the forest, she said to herself: *If, by chance, the fay were only a woman like me, I could compete in amour with her, and I love him so much that I might perhaps prevail... Then again, if she isn't a fay, she will have deceived Abel in telling him that she was making sacrifices, and I've never deceived Abel...*

Forming a thousand projects thus, hoping and creating a bright future, she did not perceive the length of the journey. She traversed the entire forest, and the marks of the wheels led her to a magnificent château, surrounded by a park, illustrious in its magnificence and picturesque aspects, the waters and rare flowers that ornamented it.

She recognized immediately the château in which the Duchesse de Sommerset lived, and a vague idea that the fay could not be anyone but that young widow celebrated for her intelligence, her beauty, and even more so for her wealth and benevolence, occurred to Catherine's mind.

The Duchesse de Sommerset received everyone with affability. Catherine asked to see her, and no one made any difficulty about introducing her.

Catherine trembled in all her limbs as she traversed the courtyards, the stairways and the apartments. Finally, having arrived at the principal drawing room, a young chambermaid, whom she recognized as the djinni of the lamp, opened the door of the boudoir that Abel had described to her.

She looked at the duchesse, recognized the fay, and fainted.

Immediately, the duchesse lavished the customary cares upon her, and when the pretty peasant girl came round, she asked her several questions with a kindness that went straight to the heart.

"Oh, Madame!" Catherine exclaimed, in the voice of despair, "your wealth, your power, nothing, nothing in the world, nothing can soothe me!"

"But what's the matter, my child?"

"Oh, Madame, I've seen you! That's sufficient; about the rest, I must maintain the most profound silence. People say that you're good, benevolent—well, what I would say to you would poison your happiness at its source. Go, adieu, Madame, be happy! However, it was me who saw him first! He belonged to me!" She put her hand over her mouth. "Oh! Let's keep, let's keep my secret, and die with it..."

The astonished duchesse contemplated the young peasant tenderly, already feeling sorry for her, while ignorant of the cause of the tears she was shedding.

In the end, the sole grace that Catherine asked was that Madame la Duchesse should have her taken back in a carriage to the village of V***.

The duchesse ordered the satisfaction of Catherine's desire, and at the same time, she gave secret instructions to her servants that they should discover the adventure that had brought the young woman to the château.

If you are curious to know by what circumstance the Duchesse de Sommerset came to be the Pearl Fay, you can cast your eyes over two letters that we have extracted from her correspondence with one of her friends.

These letters will hasten the conclusion of this adventure.

The duchesse had been living in Joigny[14] for a year; she had become bored there, and had already made trips of Paris; it was during one of those trips that she had linked herself in amity with the person to whom the letter is addressed.

Letter from the Duchesse de Sommerset
to Madame la Marquise de Stainville

Château de Joigny, ****

You complain, my dear about my retreat, my silence and my apathy, but no woman has ever been more occupied than me. As I have confided my entire life to you, I see no reason why I should not tell you, under the sworn secrecy that one keeps for at least twenty-four hours in Paris, about the adventure that retains me in the depth of the woods twelve leagues from the capital.

The folly of my entire life, my dream, is to be loved for myself. There was a time once when I thought I had achieved my goal, but the Duc de Sommerset deceived me very cruelly, by showing me that ambition, self-regard and wounded vanity do not even pardon amour. You French women, who love for a witty remark, or a beautiful leg, who, love, in sum with our head more often than your heart, will never understand...there are exceptions, I think, so, the majority of women will never understand the torture of a heart for which vanity, the

---

[14] Joigny is in the département of the Yonne, on the edge of the Forêt d'Othe. It is not obvious why the author has located the duchesse's residence there, but it might have something to do with the fact that the nearby commune of Villecien is the location of the so-called Château du Fey.

petty triumphs of self-esteem, balls and city are nothing, and which only aspires to that profound admiration, hat perpetual abasement, which composes a true sentiment.

On the death of Lord Sommerset, and even before, I sensed the void in my soul and was no longer alive; in effect, my live was devoid of charm. What is a woman's life? It is an eternal need for love; it is to be incessantly occupied with the happiness of an individual who is not her; she has a mass of sentiment that it is necessary for us to throw, at every instant, over some creature, and that mass comprises respect joy, grandeur, purity, exaltation; in sum, all of nature.

In churches, on feast days, there are children who carry baskets full of roses, and who are only occupied in strewing the flowers in the places by which the Lord might pass; that is the image of the life of a woman. We have made them proud and apparent queens, but if the one who loves sincerely re-enters into the depths of her heart, she will find for her Lord an obedience, a dread and a real servitude. To love, it is necessary to believe in perfection, and to find it in the individual one adores; he is a God, for amour is a terrestrial religion. Now, we can only be slaves of a being we see thus; everything bears us to that because everything bears us to render happy those we love.

Listen, dear friend; I am English, and in consequence a lover of reverie and extreme sentiments. Well, what I am describing to you I have in my soul: a smile from the being I cherish is a tender feast; a word makes me shiver; and I await that smile, that word, as an Arab in the desert looks out for a drop of water. That sweet occupation of always seeking to render life pleasant for a being one adores is my essence. What pleasure there is in annihilating oneself in another soul than one's own, feeling his pain, his dolor, his voluptuousness! We are born for that, for we have one sense more than men; it is the sense of instinct that bears us to please them. In sum, dear friend, I don't know how certain women contrive to shake off that nucleus of amour that they all must have.

Well, I have found a being to whom I am attaching that mass of sentiment, that vivacity of thought; that is what is retaining me in the country. Oh, my story was amusing at first, but now it's serious to the highest degree, for it's a matter of marriage.

Can you imagine that the curé of one of the villages nearby had come to pay me a visit, and that he spoke to me over dessert about a young madman who lived on a hill of his village; the young man believed in the existence of fays, and he had not yet made the acquaintance of society, had never left his cottage.

Suddenly, the idea came to me of amusing myself with that singular being, and after obtaining a great deal of information, going around his cabin by night, I noticed that there is a rather chimney wide enough to descend into the interior. Then I ordered a sumptuous costume, without forgetting my wand, and one night I embarked in a carriage, which I stopped in the forest. Fearful of the rain I had myself carried in a chair to the chimney.

Dear friend, I appeared to the sounds of beautiful music…but I found the most handsome individual that it is possible to see, and his first glance convinced me that I had found my master. I went to laugh and play, to amuse myself, but I found amour with all its magical force. I went to enchant, and it was me who was enchanted,

There are no follies that I have not committed. I have given that young man a superb fête, with illuminations, music, etc. It was believed at the time that the fête was for Lord V***, but I alone and my servants, who maintain the strictest secrecy, knew the veritable hero, whom I subjected to rude ordeals. In fact, by a hazard that served my designs, the aqueduct that once brought water to the park has an immense manhole not far from his cottage. I moved quickly to have the tunnel cleared, and he only came to the fête after being subject to a few phantasmagorical tricks and fought phantoms that were created for him. The boudoir that you admired so much was constructed uniquely for him, for on seeing me with pearls, he had named me the Pearl Fay.

I have, as you can imagine, wanted to sustain my dignity; hence, enchantments. I had one of my servants dress in his father's clothes; the places where they were worn indicated his pose, his gestures, his attitude, and in a mirror, he has seen his father, dead for a long time.

He took it into his head to believe that my night-lamp was a talisman; I had my chambermaid dress as a djinni, and she played the role marvelously. I got her to read Shakespeare's *Tempest*, and she grasped the role of Ariel very well. A machine was fitted beneath the man-hole, and every time he rapped thereon, his desires were satisfied. I had everything that he might desire brought, and for the rest, there are relays in the forest, and some-one comes to tell me immediately all that he wishes. There are also relays on the road to Paris, and in that center of civilization I obtain very rapidly, at a price of gold, what he desires. My people have orders to obey everything that the possessor of the lamp wishes, and I have made sure of their devotion and discretion.

A fortnight ago he made me run around all the min-istries for positions; fortunately, Lord V***'s credit was very useful to me, and I obtained everything in a trice.

But the completion of happiness is that he loves me as much, and perhaps even more, than I love him, for I have succeeded in confounding myself thus before him. He has the purest soul and the most loving heart in the body of an angel of heaven; his gaze is celestial; in sum, he is so modest and so tender that he realizes the ideal that my imagination had designed. He is one of the fortunate creatures of amour and happiness, a kind of flower that one rarely encounters on earth, and it has required the bizarre circumstances that have surrounded his life until now to bring a man to that perfection of nature.

Oh, he is the living proof of the principle that consecrates the innate bounty and beauty of humankind. All the generous sentiments compose the flower of his soul, in which no evil can grow. How could one not love and cherish such a creature? So I have attached all my life to that dear Abel—for Abel is his name, and expresses very will his resemblance with that first just man on earth.

Don't believe, after what I've told you, that he is as soft-headed as a sheep; he is fine and intelligent; his language is exalted, and has something Oriental about it— with the different, nevertheless, that it is often energetic and concise, like that of a natural man who only expresses ideas.

Can you conceive now how one can remain buried in the woods? But dear friend, I have one dread, and it is to you that I am addressing myself in order to put an end to it. I'm afraid, if I marry him, that all Paris will mock me. The Duchesse de Sommerset is to marry? Who? Monsieur Abel...a young man devoid of fortune and devoid of education! It's true that he will soon know as much as I want him to know. I have only to bring his books in Greek and Latin and tell him that it's necessary for him to study the language of djinn, and he'll quickly learn it for love of me—but what do Greek and Latin matter to a woman of my rank, who only wants to live for him and will not suffer other beings to approach him?

Yes, I want his life to be an eternal enchantment; I want to consecrate myself to his happiness, to erect a barrier between the world and him, that he should remain as if in a sanctuary, and forbid the approach of anything that might cause him pain or dolor, while trying nevertheless to ensure that the perpetual enchantment has nothing insipid about it.

Divine melancholy, benevolence, tears shed over the misfortune of others will not be banished from our temple; for I find that after having wept thus, one has added a greater portion of soul of soul to one's soul. I shall not even trust my amour and the multiplicity of sensations to avoid ennui, disgust and the other harpies of existence that wither everything; pleasant study, the arts and the sciences will succeed the intoxication of society, and the country salons, in the same way that in nature, autumn succeeds summer, and spring winter.

Oh, I shall marry him, for I feel that I am worthy of him; he has named me his fay; I shall be that always, and always heap him with tenderness and testimonies of my gratitude. What a life! What happiness! Oh, his love has rendered me the happiest of women, and there is no joy on earth that can compare to mine: it comes from heaven!

What reassures me about the marriage I'm planning is that ten days thereafter, people in Paris will no longer be talking about it, for you only have a certain dose of attention, and if people only talk about the fall of a great empire for six days, I can't see why anyone should bother about my union for more than two nights.

I am so crazy that, seeing Abel happy in believing me to be a fay, I dare not undeceive him.

Adieu; I await your response, etc. etc.

Letter from Madame de Stainville

One of our poets, a charming man, I don't know which, has written these divine lines:

> ....*Marry as soon as possible;*
> *Tomorrow if you can; today if you must.*

I don't know whether I'm writing them accurately,[15] but such as they are, they form the best prescription that any doctor has ever written; it is cheerful in style, in conformity with the malady. What! You fear what people will say? What do you expect Parisians to say about one of the most beautiful women in England, when she has an annual income of fifty thousand pounds sterling, except that what she has done is delightful? Yes, my friend, if you didn't put on a hat and went out bareheaded, it would become the fashion; with regard to dress codes, olives, girdles and Scottish tartans are out, we no longer wear them.

I would dearly like to know whether there are many forests in France where husbands like yours grow—for I see you already married; I've already thought about the dress that I shall have made; it will be divine, as gracious as your manner of envisaging amour, although I think

---

[15] They are in fact, accurately quoted, from Jean Racine's one and only comedy *Les Plaideurs* (1668); the advice is offered to the hero, Léandre, by his father, the magistrate Dandin—whose name implies that he is a silly fool.

you are dragging us down. My knees are the part of my delicate body that I spare the most, and I would be ashamed to be in contemplation thus before my husband. If he is in my arms, so be it, I'll try to make him comfortable there, poor man, but me at his knees! Fie on that! You're abasing us too much by pitting men so high. Personally, I imagine that men are to some extent made for us, and that their life ought to receive its flame from us; the proof that they're made for our usage is that we are mothers, and in consequences the mistresses of the world.

Having been very stupidly married and loving my husband in order to do as everyone does, since I mean to say everything that the spirit of our century holds to be the case...in any case, he's a worthy man, and I wouldn't want to cause him pain for thirty lovers! Where was I? Oh, yes...I nevertheless married very stupidly, in that I was twenty-two and Monsieur le Marquis was forty-nine, which means that when I'm thirty he'll be fifty-seven, if my arithmetic is correct; now, can you imagine that I can "pour my sensibility" over a sexagenarian, "attach my life" to him and "occupy myself with his happiness"? While he takes a pinch of snuff I'll have a thousand thoughts; when he climbs into one carriage door, I'll get out through the other; in truth, the future frightens me, and I think you're very lucky to be marrying a handsome young man whom you love. Nevertheless, poor Stainville has qualities, I love him—but listen to me, for I'll shout it very loudly in writing my last word to you: *marry!*

Has your little Abel a moustache? Can he ride a horse? Does he know Rossini, Lord Byron? What are his habits? Does he tilt his head, does he walk straight or do his steps stutter, like our old people? You haven't given me any details about his person. But I think, my dear, that you've calumniated the French horribly in saying that they only love with the head; think and about it, and you'll reform that judgment, on seeing Madame S***, Madame G*** etc., who have had so many lovers and are so agreeable.

I'm going to the Bouffes this evening; I always think of you when I see your empty box; people ask me for news of you, and I tell everyone that you're in the provinces to put a little lead in your spirit, because you were crushing everyone with your amiability, and that you only want to make enemies because of your beauty. Think about it, my dear—you're going to lose a great deal in that solitude. Come back to Paris soon—without that, no salvation.

I've reflected on what you say about the need that women have to throw their sensibility over something, and I'm laughing like a lunatic, because I have a little monkey that I love passionately, since a fortnight ago, and what will enable me to love my husband forever is that I have a weakness for poor animals; that preserves me from betraying conjugal fidelity, in that my sensibility will be exercised on some animal. Oh, I'm profoundly philosophical and I haven't, for five years, been sowing, embroidering, painting water colors, skimming my piano-keys and warbling songs without knowing a thing or two. Adieu, dear friend...

P.S. Poppy-red is in vogue; I write that for your guidance; all will be lost if Abel doesn't see you in poppy-red. Oh, what a pretty name Abel is! Are you glad to be able to combine it with a tender name, like "my dear Abel" or "my sweet Abel" without it sounding ridiculous? That's another advantage I lost with Stainville, as calling him my sweet Marc, my dear Marc, would swear too much; it's like combining satin with the fabric from which judges' and prosecutors' robes are made...

Adieu, dear Jenny...Jenny! In a little while, we'll be saying Abel and Jenny!

Chapter XIV
Catherine's Adieux

For some time poor Catherine was prey to a chagrin so profound that she did not emerge from her modest room, and pretended to be ill, which was easy to believe because of the alteration of her tender physiognomy.

One morning, however, she got up, wanting to go for a walk, and headed slowly toward the hill, for one last smile of hope had sustained her: *The duchesse is very beautiful, but that being said, she has deceived Abel, and I'll see what Abel thinks about that.*

She went up the tortuous path to the cottage languidly, arrived in Abel's company, and a soft pinkness mingled with the pallor of her face. Abel was on the stone, making his projects for the future—for he could not doubt his happiness, and he was only thinking about rendering the fay the happiest of fays.

I shall try, he said to himself, *to go far away with her, far from djinn and humans. We shall be in a beautiful palace, surrounded by delightful gardens; there, unknown and content, I shall be the most devoted and most attentive slave to her. In the same way that she poured me ambrosia in her divine abode some time ago, I shall watch out for her needs—if fays have any—her thoughts and her desires. To carry out her orders will be my delight, a glance my greatest joy; in sum, she will be a kind of visible deity that I shall adore incessantly; our thoughts and wishes will be the same, and my life will be all amour.*

At that point, Catherine appeared.

"Oh, Catherine!" said Abel. "How changed you are! What's the matter?"

"Abel," she replied, sitting down beside him, "you're very lucky to love a fay."

"Oh yes."

"It's that quality of being a fay, that brilliant power, that prestige, which charms you."

"Yes, Catherine; I shall fly with her on the clouds; my sentiments will be purified in the high regions of the sky—O joy!"

"Well," Catherine continued, prey to a cruel doubt, "what if your fay weren't a fay, if she were only a woman like me...if she had deceived you..."

Abel remained mute, his eyes expressing by turns a host of various sentiments, and poor Catherine consulted his face, as a criminal awaiting sentence consults the eyes of the jurors coming out of the room of their deliberations. Her heart was beating with an astonishing force and rapidity: joy first, then doubt, then joy...but finally, the greatest chagrin agitated her, for Abel ended up exclaiming:

"Oh, dear Catherine, what idea are you daring to present to me? If she were...well, I would be the happiest of men, for she would no longer be above me. I feel in my heart so much love, such a great consciousness of strength, that she would then obtain her happiness from me. Her power made me adore her, her weakness would render her even more precious to me. Oh, Catherine, may you be telling the truth!"

"You'll soon find out," the young peasant replied, getting up, "and in a little while, you'll receive the adieux of your little Catherine; then you'll know me...for in the brilliant society into which the Duchesse de Sommerset, your genteel fay, will draw you...Catherine would be out of place...what am I saying? She would harm your happiness, for you're too sensible not to feel sorry for me; but I'll try to make sure that my memory doesn't trouble your prosperity. Abel, I can't complain about our choice, for the duchesse merits being loved...she eclipses all the women on earth. Adieu, Abel."

"What you're saying to me makes me shiver," he replied. "What a tone!" After a moment's silence, he exclaimed: "You think big!"

"Shh!" she said, placing a pretty finger over his lips. "I only ask one favor of you, which is not to leave the cottage without having received Catherine's adieu... Adieu; I can hear a carriage in the distance...it's her; it's the duchesse. Adieu!"

She fled through the rocks, with the gait of a creature deprived of reason.

Indeed, as she had said, a brilliant caleche arrived in front of the cottage, and the Duchesse de Sommerset descended from it.

Abel received her in his arms and exclaimed: "Catherine has just told me that you're not a fay."

"No, she replied, "for fays don't exist; they're an imaginary creation."

"What are you, then?"

"More than a fay," she said.

"What?" asked Abel, with a keen curiosity.

"I am," she said, embracing her beloved, "a woman in love! Who is consecrating herself to your existence, who will try to embellish it, who is sacrificing rank, fortune, honors and prejudices, burning all human vanities like an incense scarcely worthy of the altar of amour. Your naïve soul cannot know society as yet, its bizarreries and its distinctions. One day, Abel, you'll understand the kind of sacrifice I'm making for you; you'll even be astonished that a woman of the world has done it; but seeing every day how much I love you, you'll find it quite simple.

"If I were to tell you that I'm a duchesse, that I have an income in excess of a million, you wouldn't be any the wiser. You don't have anything, except for the one thing that can't be bought: a beautiful soul, of which all the pure, harmonious sounds resonate like an echo of heaven.

"See, I'm discarding any sentiment of coquetry; it's futile with the pupil of nature; I'm coming to you, taking you by the hand, placing it against my heart—which it completes—depositing an amorous kiss on your lips and telling you, with the naivety you have in your soul, and of which I only have a reflection: 'Abel, I love you, would you like to walk with me in life? I will always smile at you; when you fall asleep on the route, I shall stay awake in order to extend branches over your head and prevent the insects from troubling your sleep; the path will always be strewn with flowers; your life will be a continuous enchantment, and I shall try to be always a fay to you."

Abel was kneeling before the duchesse, his head confounded with the feet of the charming woman, and tears were dampening the elegant cothurnes she was wearing.

"Get up, Abel; it's to my heart that it's necessary to come."

She sat down beside him.

"Would you like me to take you away," she said, smiling, "and quit this cottage today in order to come and live in my house—yours, that is to say, for everything is yours."

"Oh, dear fay—yes, fay, that name will always remain yours—can I quit this place so suddenly? How can I abandon Caliban, and Catherine my loving sister, without saying adieu, and go to live in cities with you? My father told me that then I had to lift the stone in the fireplace, and that I'd find a talisman there."

"Well, my dear Abel, I'll leave you until tomorrow. But tomorrow, my love, my heaven, permit me to come and take you away from this place, and enjoy your gaze and your presence forever..."

"Yes, yes," said Abel, at the peak of his joy.

After having spent a delightful morning together, one of those moments in which the soul alone overflows, in which one has, in a way, a double existence, the duchesse quit her husband-to-be, and left him intoxicated by happiness.

He said to Caliban: "Old friend, I give you my cabin and my garden; be happy here. Every year I shall come to see you; I shall give you someone to be your Caliban beside you, as you were for me. Conserve the cottage carefully, all of my father respires here. His soul seems to have taken refuge in those furnaces; his grave is nearby; this place ought to be sacred; nothing should profane it.

Caliban said to him: "If you are to be happy, Abel, go. But your father was wise, and he wanted you to stay here: fear that society is not worth as much as this solitude..."

Together, they lifted the stone in the fireplace, and found a heavy coffer. Their surprise was extreme on opening it, for it was full of diamonds of the greatest beauty, either because they had been made by the chemist or because he had realized his fortune in that fashion.

"Oh!" Abel exclaimed. "If I could be as rich as her!"

There were old parchments with the diamonds. After having read them, Abel found that he had another name than that of Abel, and that name was Comte Osterwald. How indignant a recent ennobled man would be on learning that that discovery could not make Abel feel anything!

Caliban went to the village; he went to the Maire's house and told Catherine that Abel would be leaving tomorrow with the Duchesse de Sommerset. She was by the fireside, playing in a melancholy fashion with the jet necklace, her greatest treasure. Her father, whom she no longer entertained with her sweet songs, was asleep.

When Caliban had gone, she hid her face in her hands and started to weep. Overwhelmed with questions by her father, who had woken up, she did not want to answer any of them, and when she heard Jacques Bontems coming, she withdrew precipitately, because she did not want anyone to witness her dolor.

The next morning, she went to the cottage. She was dressed exactly as he had been when she saw Abel for the first time. She went into the cottage, but as soon as she had crossed the threshold she dissolved in tears. She sat down in the worm-eaten armchair and looked at Abel, unable to speak.

The young man drew near and took her by the hand—which she let him take—and he said to her: "Catherine, I'm going to leave this place, but you're going to stay here, so be sure that I'll come back often— unless you prefer to come with me...."

"Come with you! Abel, Abel, I'll accompany you with my soul; I'll follow you everywhere. Know, then— it would have been finer to keep quiet, but that effort is beyond my strength—that I love you amorously, that I will never love anyone but you, that your fraternal affection is nothing...what am I saying?...it's everything, but it's still not enough. For a long time I've been drying up in tears; I'm losing you forever, but I can't forget you. How unhappy I am, Abel! Reason told me that it couldn't be otherwise, but my heart still hoped..."

Sobs prevented her from going on.

"Oh, Catherine!" cried Abel. "You're breaking my heart! How I want you to be happy! What is necessary for that? It's said that in society, riches are something for happiness. Here, Catherine, take them..." And seizing a handful of large diamonds, he poured them over Catherine.

"Abel!" she cried, weeping. "Is that worthy of you? Can anything console a heart deprived of the one it loves?" And with a movement of scorn and indignation as rapid as thought, she stood up, threw the diamonds on the ground, and, looking at Abel with an admirable tenderness full of profound dolor, she said to him: "Give me, just give me one loving kiss, and even the tomb will seem charming to me! Kiss me to say adieu, and that simple, chaste caress will be more to me than all the world, more than the heavens!"

Abel gripped her by her slender waist and deposited a tender kiss on her burning lips...

Catherine went pale, and fainted, saying: "That's fire! Oh, I've lived!"

Catherine, pale and almost dead, was in Abel's arms when the duchesse came in...

"Madame," said Catherine, recovering her senses, "may you be forever ignorant of what your happiness has cost me."

She looked at Abel, contemplated him, carried him away entire in her heart, and disappeared.

Abel, left alone with the fay, told her everything that his father had done for him, and the duchesse was at the peak of delight when she learned that Abel was a Comte and worth millions. That joy came from the fact that she saw all conveniences coming together, and that the marriage would give less purchase to malicious talk.

Would Catherine have had that surge of joy?

Poor Catherine went to her father's house. There, Jacques Bontems and Grandvani pressed her to consent to the marriage, and the young woman, looking at the cuirassier, made a frightful movement of the head as a sign of assent....

That movement...I can only compare it to that of the head of a skeleton detaching itself from the body.

They looked at her, wondering with their eyes: *What's the matter with her, then?*

The joy disappeared; Catherine's color faded away; she became distracted; she wandered rather than walking. Often, she gazed without seeing.

Meanwhile, in Paris, the Duchesse de Sommerset's adventure was on all lips. Their marriage decided, the two fiancés would not wait for long. It was the same in the village.

Chapter XV
The Two Weddings

In Paris, in the Duchesse of Sommerset's magnificent town house, a joyful crowd inundated all the rooms; the most sumptuous costumes, the prettiest women, important men and a multitude of strangers shone with a splendid glare. Every room in the house, in the reception apartments, was decorated with several chandeliers ornamented by a multitude of candles that were reflected by a thousand mirrors. The most precious and most elegant items of furniture, silks of a hundred colors, brilliant satins, precious porcelains, gilded ornaments, sculpted bronzes, crystals full of artificial flowers and perfumes—everything, in sum, that the most frenzied luxury of modernity has been able to invent of the exquisite, the voluptuous and the delicate—was brought together in that palace, and offered as a trophy to ornament the temple of the happiest marriage that had ever been contracted.

Flocking, on the word of Renown, to contemplate the chemist's son with the millions, the charming, noble and rich hero of his adventure, the numerous friends of the duchesse and many strangers flooded the house. The Place Vendôme was encumbered by a hot of carriages each more brilliant than the next, and there was an immense assembly of domestics under the peristyle and in the courtyard.

In one of the galleries of the house a sumptuous feast was being prepared; the walls of the gallery were ornamented with paintings by the most famous masters, and the curious could not tear themselves away from the contemplation of that magnificent gallery, worthy of a sovereign. Several of them, doubtless gastronomes, reposed their admiration, settling it on the organization of a long table on which silverware glittered, along with candles, plates, magical decorations, the most sought-after foodstuffs—the latest productions of luxury—sculptures and vases, all masterpieces of art. It was a veritable enchantment.

In the principal salon, amid a thousand beauties, Jenny de Sommerset, wearing the rich costume of the Pearl Fay, eclipsed everyone else; she attracted all gazes; her vivid beauty, her grace, her seductiveness, rendered her the object of all desires; and, in the same way that everything in nature in related to the sun, everything in the hearts and visages of the guests only lived by virtue of her, and were combined in her. She was the center of a multitude of radii.

As for Comte Osterwald, he reigned as a sovereign over the fay, as his fay reigned over everything else. One could not call what was happening at that moment in his being "living"; all the women were admiring him, and there was no one who did not agree that there was reason to do so, for Abel, in the midst of the most handsome men who surrounded him, made himself remarkable, and prevailed, by the expression of happiness that emerged from every pore of his celestial visage. An angelic candor, a gentle pride, a moist and magical gaze, hair floating in rounded jet-black curls, elegant and pure forms, and that naïve and naturally casual bearing, rendered him a living image of the famous Greek statuary in which all human perfections are assembled.

Abel found himself transplanted from the bosom of the ignorant life of nature to the summit of civilization, into the midst of all that society offers of the most seductive; he was accompanied by the woman he loved and enjoyed the superhuman voluptuousness of seeing her the queen of her circle; he sensed that everyone envied him his happiness, and his ideas had acquired sufficient extension for him to perceive that, at that moment, he was the sole individual among fifty million human beings who had such a sensation, with which all the forces of creation seemed to concur.

In fact, the most harmonious music have the signal for that celebration, and Abel remained plunged therein in a cloud of voluptuous sensation so renascent that his soul no longer had the strength to do anything but feel; he was no longer able to think; he gazed incessantly at that profusion of wealth, and always came to confound his sight in the enchanting aspect of his dear little fay, who intoxicated him with the most delicate, the most amorous and the sweetest glances. Everything was smiling at them; the entire universe was poring over their amour. No tales of enchantment had ever given the image of such a fête. In sum, he was all enjoyment, and had not sufficient eyes to see or soul to feel.

How, then, could he have thought about Catherine?

Catherine, the poor child! Her name recalls us to the village. We know the modest abode of Père Grandvani: that kitchen so clean and so cluttered, and Françoise scarcely sufficient to direct the ovens. The Maire's room has been cleared of the furniture that once garnished it; on the table where Catherine's needlework once lay, one sees the Maire's modest white faience crockery. A few white porcelain cups, poorly served fruits, scant silverware, but a frank cheerfulness on all faces: that is what one perceives.

The sergeant of the cuirassiers of the guard is there, his uniform shiny with his medal, as large as a half-franc coin; he turns up his moustache, and thinks profoundly on seeing Catherine. The poor girl is in front of the modest fireplace. Juliette is putting the finishing touches to her costume and attaching the virginal bouquet to it. Catherine is pale; she gazes without seeing; her lips are colorless; they are slightly parted, and a painful breath escapes between her white teeth. The adornment that she has put on is that which *he* gave her.

Catherine tries to put on one of her gloves, but cannot do it. Three times her hand has passed through the opening of the white glove; she looks, lamentably, at Juliette, who sheds a tear, for poor Catherine has as eyes as dry as Brutus when he saw his dead sons.[16]

Père Grandvani contemplates his daughter; he examines her, and an involuntary fear takes possession of his senses. He dares not speak; he can only gaze at his dear daughter. Bontems is silent, perhaps thinking that the testimonies of his amour will make that excess of modesty—the last regret of a girl saying a virginal adieu to the nature of her childhood—disappear. He consoles Père Grandvani thus, and because hope is the most persuasive god, the poor Maire is deceived.

---

[16] The reference is to a painting in the Louvre by Jacques-Louis David, *Les licteurs rapportent à Brutus les corps de ses fils* (1789). The French Revolution broke out before that year's Salon was opened, and when the newspapers reported that the painting had been proscribed because of its Republican symbolism—Brutus being a staunch defender of the Roman Republic—there was an outcry; it was hung regardless, defended by a cordon of art students, and thus become legendary.

Before leaving the room to go to the church, Catherine went to her father, put her arms around him, and deposited a filial kiss on his forehead imprinted with all the love she had for him. The poor father blessed her with a smile.

They go in silence to the church. Everything is a dream for Catherine; she kneels down mechanically and gives her hand to the priest, as if by instinct.

The curé found it cold; he looked at Catherine, and trembled involuntarily.

The wedding party returned to Père Grandvani's house, accompanied by two violins and a joyful troop. Every peasant had a knot of ribbons on his buttonhole, for the entire village adored Catherine.

An old woman sitting under an enormous elm saw the cortege pas by; she darted a horrified glance at the bride, and whispered to another old woman who was sitting beside her: "That bride will die a virgin!"

Grandvani's room received the guests. Juliette and Catherine went up the antique staircase together and went into Catherine's virginal bedroom. The room maintained an extreme propriety; on going into it, one divined, but the care that reigned there, that the charming being who inhabited that simple place decorated with white cambric and modest furniture, was a being composed of love and tenderness: there was not a single speck of dust; a spirit of order and goodness murmured that the young virgin remained pure, and that her thoughts, as naïve as her, had only ever had one object.

"Juliette" she said, "I love God, but I love *him* almost as much. It's necessary not to deceive anyone down here; I can't live with Jacques, and life is nothing without the gifts of a shared love. I prefer a dagger-thrust to a thousand pinpricks during my life. I only have *him* in my heart, as you know. It's not because his face is beautiful for if he had been ugly I would have been even more content to look at him. He's happy now. Well, I'll be on high to make sure that nothing is lacking to his happiness."

Juliette wept.

"You're weeping, my dear sister?" Stop—don't mourn me. *He* told me that there are divine spirits that become dew, which are the coloring of flowers, the morning breeze, the evening star, which glide through the air distributing sounds. I shall be one of those, and I shall always remain close to *him*. Adieu, Juliette,"

"Oh, let me hope," said Antoine's wife.

"Yes," said Catherine, "hope! For I hope myself; perhaps all is not yet concluded...."

They separated, weeping, and Catherine deposited a tender kiss of hope or adieu on her friend's lips.

Juliette went downstairs; she found the guests around the table; she took her place, everyone was joyful; the feasting began; the dancing was to follow, but Jacques Bontems and Grandvani noticed that Catherine was missing.

The guests looked at one another in silence, and Juliette said to herself: *No more joy!*

However, for some time yet, they continued eating and laughing—but the intrepid cuirassier felt his heart faltering, and the father, as he poured the wine, trembled so much that it spilled over the table.

In the end, he asked for his daughter; someone went to fetch her—but she could not be found.

Horror and silence reigned in the formerly joyful house, and nothing could any longer be heard but the pendulum of the clock measuring the instants of anguish and terror.

Juliette, who had promised secrecy, tried to appear as anxious as the rest.

The house emptied. Grandvani, Bontems and Juliette were left alone, surrounded by the cortege of dolor, silence and dread.

Grandvani was still looking at the door, and when Françoise opened it, he shivered, but he only felt a dolor even more profound, because it was not his daughter. The village was in stupor.

Meanwhile, in the middle of the night, when the most voluptuous dances accompanied by an enchanting music had given scope to Abel's wife and her rivals to deploy everything their bodies had of the most supple and enchanting; when the brilliant fête was fatigued by the very abundance of wealth and splendor, it was announced that a sumptuous meal awaited the thousand guests.

The excessive heat had caused a few windows in the house to be opened. At the moment when someone came to announce to Madame le Duchesse that dinner was served, Abel was breathing in the fresh nocturnal air.

"Are you coming, then, dear friend?" said his bride, who, seeing that he was not quitting the balcony, put her hand lightly on his shoulder and tugged him gently.

"Can you not see something out there?" Abel replied.

She advanced her head, and they both perceived a white mass that the obscurity, slightly tempered by the lanterns, only permitted to be seen in an indistinct manner. By dint of looking, they saw the mass move, taking shape in the darkness and allowing forms to appear; it was a woman.

She was wandering, raising herself up on tiptoe, being to be allowed to enter. Suddenly, she looked up at the casement, and immersed herself in the contemplation of the two charming individuals whose contours the light of the salon seemed to caress in rendering them graspable to sight.

Abel assembled his memories; he thought…was not sure…that it was Catherine…but there was certainly something that resembled her; he thought he recognized the costume of Juliette's wedding. He hesitated…

His charming bride, on the pretext that everyone was waiting, drew him away.

Then, when he quit the window, dolorous accents, the debris of a charming voice, reached his ear: there were wishes for his happiness…a joy at having seen him…albeit from afar and in a fugitive manner…and then regrets…amour, and finally an adieu spoken with the voice of death.

The woman waved her arms toward him for a long time, and uttered a cry when he disappeared.

The momentum of the fête, the joy of the nuptial meal, the enchantments of the miraculous gallery, the presence of a crowd prey to joy, made that instant of trouble a dreamlike moment, almost forgotten, for Abel.

The last outbursts of joy were resounding in the salons when Abel and the Pearl Fay had withdrawn. Abel was swimming in a torrent of delights, without worrying about whether, elsewhere, people were living or dying, happy or unhappy, whether pain and chagrin might be devouring sensitive beings; an immense sum had just been spent; it had just vanished in enjoyments of pride—light smoke!—in wines, foodstuffs, witty remarks, subjects of indigestions and indiscretions…

But if one thought about that, one would not take any pleasure in the world, one would always be weeping!

Long live joy! Down with chagrin!

Jacques Bontems spent his wedding night running around the village; he had death in his soul and offered to give his sight for news of Catherine. No one had seen her.

Grandvani would have given all his wealth for a curl of his dear Catherine's hair; she was his only child, his joy and his happiness. He saw his house empty; the pretty Catherine, so genteel, so lovable, so good was no longer there!

Dolor filled that entire night.

Two days after his marriage, Abel, drunk with joy and happiness, at the peak of human enjoyment, was borne away by an elegant carriage on the road to Versailles, which the duchesse wanted to take him to see, for that charming fay surrounded Abel with all seductions. She unveiled all the riches of the capital to him, spreading the grace of her intelligence in all her discourse, seeking to cover with flowers the roads that Abel traveled. Their hands were united, pressing one another amorously, and a caleche harnessed to six horses rolled with frightening rapidity along the banks of the Seine.

A group of three individuals, a soldier, a peasant woman and an old man, were being studied by a saddened crowd, because the dolor of those individuals was so true and so profound that it had spread from person to person; their movements were imprinted by the slowness that one put into the accomplishment of a painful duty; it seemed that their fatigued arms fell back continually.

A young woman had just been taken out of the water. Her garments were so tight around her body that there was nothing to be done other than take her as the fatal net had stopped her in the bosom of the waters. Only her hair was floating...and she was holding between her teeth, with the force that death gives, a black necklace with which she had doubtless wanted to perish and be buried.

The caleche went past very rapidly, but the fleeting glance that the tender Abel darted at the group made him shiver, for that hair, that figure, and above all that familiar necklace, told him: "It's your sister in amour; it's Catherine!"

But the caleche carried him away so quickly that he was already far away, very far, when having recovered from his double surprise, he cried: "Stop! I want to see her again!"

The caleche was still going on, for the tender fay, fearing chagrins for him, divining that he was about to seek a dolor, was too careful of drawing the thorns of life from him to suffer that his heart might break, and a movement of her delicate hand ordered the coachman to go even faster.

Poor Catherine!

When, after a year of marriage, Comte Osterwald went back to see his cottage and Caliban, he perceived before the door a grave covered with grass, in the middle of which, without inscription and without ostentation, a young lily was growing proudly.

Abel, looking at the comtesse, exclaimed: "Poor Catherine!"

Caliban appeared, carrying a watering can; he was walking painfully, with the air of a shade; it was him who watered the lily, and he often said: "She loved him, she...!" He did not add anything more, for the old servant had lost his reason, and only recognized his young master.

That reawakening of the soul, in that body near the tomb, had something moving about it; he cried: "I've seen him again; I can die!"

As he finished that speech, he dropped the watering can, he leaned over the grave, and his soul regained the heavens. As he exhaled his last sigh, his cold and icy hand made a few movements, as if to shake that of the young comte.

Thus far, the greatest joy crowns Abel's existence every day, and that cloudless happiness will doubtless endure.

Afterword
by the Translator

As noted in the introduction, *La Dernière fée* was attempting to achieve something new in prose fiction, which perhaps turned out to be impractical—at least in the sense that the story is preposterously implausible—but was nevertheless a heroic endeavor, which a close reading of the text suggests that the author seems to have pushed through to its logical conclusion even after he became convinced that it was not working. In fact, the disfavor that the story often found, both initially and thereafter, probably has little to do with its implausibility—for which subsequent literary history has demonstrated abundantly that readers have a high tolerance—and much more to do with the author's insistence of driving it relentlessly to a conclusion that, although logically necessary, is also deliberately discomfiting.

It is, of course, traditional that "fairy stories" end happily; in English the standard formula is usually rendered as "And they lived happily ever after." That is not always true of the folkloristic tales on which "fairy" stories are notionally based, but the fact that it often is reflects a common assumption that stories ought to end happily because that is the way that hearers and readers prefer them to end, and many hearers and readers feel betrayed and cheated if they do not.

Writers attempting to sophisticate folkloristic materials in stories dosed with an element of realism or cynicism, however, often want to oppose or undermine that assumption. It is not obvious why readers and writers are so often at odds over this matter—which is to say, why writers, who are also readers themselves, so often want to defy and thwart reader expectations in one way or another. Clearly the psychology of reading and the psychology of writing have a significant difference that warrants investigation. It is, however, manifestly the case that many writers, at least some of the time, do want, determinedly and passionately, to oppose the yoke that readers (and hence editors) want to place upon them by demanding happy endings, in the interests of arguing—or screaming—that the real world is *not like that*.

There are, of course, entire genres of fiction whose stories do not end happily, including the genre of tragedy—but it is worth noting that the sense of tragedy is parasitic upon the sentiment that stories ought to end happily; if it were not for that conviction, catastrophic endings would not be "tragic," but merely routine accidents of happenstance. Another such genre, generally known as *contes cruels*, was pioneered by one of Balzac's closest friends when they were both struggling writers in the early 1820s, S. Henry Berthoud, in the collection *Contes misanthropiques* (1831; tr. as *Misanthropic Tales*). Balzac wrote tales of that kind himself, and the two of them undoubtedly discussed narrative strategies appropriate to the undermining of the essential fictitiousness of conventional fiction.

That awareness helps to understand what Balzac was trying to do in *La Dernière fée*, and the way in which he did it. It is a work that sets out to fuse the conventional happy ending demanded by tales of enchantment with tragedy, by making the tragedy a necessary consequence of the happy ending, and hence a perverse aspect of it; in terms of narrative strategy, it is a matter of finding a way to sugar-coat the cake and poison it too.

The story ends, as it designed to do, with a paraphrase of "And they lived happily ever after"—although it scrupulously uses the future tense rather than the past, because the "once upon a time" in which the story is set is located in historical time, not the mythological time of tales of the marvelous, and hence leads inexorably to the present.

The whole point of the story, therefore, is to make that ostentatiously happy ending one face of a coin whose other side is stark, harrowing tragedy. It thus contrives a challenge to and a subversion of conventional reader expectation that is markedly different from tragedies and *contes cruels*, which is arguably even more brutal than tragedy and even more vitriolically ironic than a *conte cruel*. Perhaps the combination does not really work, and the narrative effort required to set it up certainly renders the story's plot implausible, but it nevertheless aims for an interesting species of discomfiture, which has few parallels even now, let alone in 1823. That alone surely makes the story with reading, and worth pondering. It is, admittedly, slightly rough-hewn work, but it is rough-hewn work by a genius, and that shows; many a polished craftsman could not have done half as well.

SF & FANTASY

Adolphe Alhaiza. *Cybele*
Alphonse Allais. *The Adventures of Captain Cap*
Henri Allorge. *The Great Cataclysm*
Guy d'Armen. *Doc Ardan: The City of Gold and Lepers; The Troglodytes of Mount Everest/The Giants of Black Lake*
G.-J. Arnaud. *The Ice Company*
André Arnyvelde. *The Ark; The Mutilated Bacchus*
Charles Asselineau. *The Double Life*
Henri Austruy. *The Eupantophone; The Olotelepan; The Petitpaon Era*
Barillet-Lagargousse. *The Final War*
Cyprien Bérard. *The Vampire Lord Ruthwen*
S. Henry Berthoud. *Martyrs of Science*
Aloysius Bertrand. *Gaspard de la Nuit*
Richard Bessière. *The Gardens of the Apocalypse; The Masters of Silence*
Chevalier de Béthune. *The World of Mercury*
Albert Bleunard. *Ever Smaller*
Félix Bodin. *The Novel of the Future*
Pierre Boitard. *Journey to the Sun*
Louis Boussenard. *Monsieur Synthesis*
Alphonse Brown. *City of Glass; The Conquest of the Air*
Émile Calvet. *In a Thousand Years*
André Caroff. *The Terror of Madame Atomos; Miss Atomos; The Return of Madame Atomos; The Mistake of Madame Atomos; The Monsters of Madame Atomos; The Revenge of Madame Atomos; The Resurrection of Madame Atomos; The Mark of Madame Atomos; The Spheres of Madame Atomos; The Wrath of Madame Atomos* (w/M. & Sylvie Stéphan)
Félicien Champsaur. *Homo-Deus; The Human Arrow; Nora, The Ape-Woman; Ouha, King of the Apes; Pharaoh's Wife*
Didier de Chousy. *Ignis*
Jules Clarétie. *Obsession*
Jacques Collin de Plancy. *Voyage to the Center of the Earth*

Michel Corday. *The Eternal Flame; The Lynx* (w/André Couvreur)

André Couvreur. *Caresco, Superman; The Exploits of Professor Tornada* (3 vols.); *The Necessary Evil*

Camille Debans. *The Misfortunes of John Bull*

Captain Danrit. *Undersea Odyssey*

C. I. Defontenay. *Star (Psi Cassiopeia)*

Charles Derennes. *The People of the Pole*

Georges Dodds (anthologist). *The Missing Link*

Charles Dodeman. *The Silent Bomb*

Harry Dickson. *The Heir of Dracula; Harry Dickson vs. The Spider*

Jules Dornay. *Lord Ruthven Begins*

Alfred Driou. *The Adventures of a Parisian Aeronaut*

Odette Dulac. *The War of the Sexes*

Alexandre Dumas. *The Return of Lord Ruthven*

Renée Dunan. *Baal; The Ultimate Pleasure*

J.-C. Dunyach. *The Night Orchid; The Thieves of Silence*

Henri Duvernois. *The Man Who Found Himself*

Achille Eyraud. *Voyage to Venus*

Henri Falk. *The Age of Lead*

Paul Féval. *Anne of the Isles; Knightshade; Revenants; Vampire City; The Vampire Countess; The Wandering Jew's Daughter*

Paul Féval, *fils. Felifax, the Tiger-Man*

Charles de Fieux. *Lamékis*

Fernand Fleuret. *Jim Click*

Louis Forest. *Someone is Stealing Children in Paris*

Arnould Galopin. *Doctor Omega; Doctor Omega and the Shadowmen* (anthology)

Judith Gautier. *Isoline and the Serpent-Flower*

H. Gayar. *The Marvelous Adventures of Serge Myrandhal on Mars*

Louis Geoffroy. *Apocryphal Napoleon*

G.L. Gick. *Harry Dickson and the Werewolf of Rutherford Grange*

Raoul Gineste. *The Second Life of Doctor Albin*

Delphine de Girardin. *Balzac's Cane*
Léon Gozlan. *The Vampire of the Val-de-Grâce*
Jules Gros. *The Fossil Man*
Jimmy Guieu. *The Polarian-Denebian War* (2 vols.)
Edmond Haraucourt. *Daah, the First Human; Illusions of Immortality*
Nathalie Henneberg. *The Green Gods*
Eugène Hennebert. *The Enchanted City*
Jules Hoche. *The Maker of Men and His Formula*
V. Hugo, P. Foucher & P. Meurice. *The Hunchback of Notre-Dame*
Romain d'Huissier. *Hexagon: Dark Matter*
Jules Janin. *The Magnetized Corpse*
Michel Jeury. *Chronolysis*
Gustave Kahn. *The Tale of Gold and Silence*
Gérard Klein. *The Mote in Time's Eye*
Fernand Kolney. *Love in 5000 Years*
Paul Lacroix. *Danse Macabre*
Louis-Guillaume de La Follie. *The Unpretentious Philosopher*
Jean de La Hire. *The Fiery Wheel; Enter the Nyctalope; The Nyctalope on Mars; The Nyctalope vs. Lucifer; The Nyctalope Steps In; Night of the Nyctalope; Return of the Nyctalope*
Etienne-Léon de Lamothe-Langon. *The Virgin Vampire*
André Laurie. *Spiridon*
Gabriel de Lautrec. *The Vengeance of the Oval Portrait*
Alain le Drimeur. *The Future City*
Georges Le Faure & Henri de Graffigny. *The Extraordinary Adventures of a Russian Scientist Across the Solar System* (2 vols.)
Gustave Le Rouge. *The Dominion of the World* (w/Gustave Guitton) (4 vols.); *The Mysterious Doctor Cornelius* (3 vols.); *The Vampires of Mars*
Jules Lermina. *The Battle of Strasbourg; Mysteryville; Panic in Paris; The Secret of Zippelius; To-Ho and the Gold Destroyers*
André Lichtenberger. *The Centaurs; The Children of the Crab*
Maurice Limat. *Mephista*

Listonai. *The Philosophical Voyager*
Jean-Marc & Randy Lofficier. *Edgar Allan Poe on Mars; The Katrina Protocol; Pacifica 1, 2; Robonocchio; Return of the Nyctalope;* (anthologists) *Tales of the Shadowmen 1-12; The Vampire Almanac* (2 vols.)
Ch. Lomon & P.-B. Gheuzi. *The Last Days of Atlantis*
Camille Mauclair. *The Virgin Orient*
Xavier Mauméjean. *The League of Heroes*
Joseph Méry. *The Tower of Destiny*
Hippolyte Mettais. *Paris Before the Deluge; The Year 5865*
Louise Michel. *The Human Microbes; The New World*
Tony Moilin. *Paris in the Year 2000*
José Moselli. *Illa's End*
John-Antoine Nau. *Enemy Force*
Marie Nizet. *Captain Vampire*
Charles Nodier. *Trilby and The Crumb Fairy*
C. Nodier, A. Beraud & Toussaint-Merle. *Frankenstein*
Henri de Parville. *An Inhabitant of the Planet Mars*
Gaston de Pawlowski. *Journey to the Land of the 4th Dimension*
Georges Pellerin. *The World in 2000 Years*
Ernest Pérochon. *The Frenetic People*
Pierre Pelot. *The Child Who Walked on the Sky*
Jean Petithuguenin. *An International Mission to the Moon*
J. Polidori, C. Nodier, E. Scribe. *Lord Ruthven the Vampire*
P.-A. Ponson du Terrail. *The Immortal Woman; The Vampire and the Devil's Son*
Georges Price. *The Missing Men of the* Sirius
René Pujol. *The Chimerical Quest*
Edgar Quinet. *Ahasuerus; The Enchanter Merlin*
Henri de Régnier. *A Surfeit of Mirrors*
Maurice Renard. *The Blue Peril; Doctor Lerne; The Doctored Man; A Man Among the Microbes; The Master of Light*
Restif de la Bretonne. *The Discovery of the Austral Continent by a Flying Man; Posthumous Correspondence* (3 vols.)
Jean Richepin. *The Crazy Corner; The Wing*

Albert Robida. *The Adventures of Saturnin Farandoul; Chalet in the Sky; The Clock of the Centuries; The Electric Life; The Engineer Von Satanas*

J.-H. Rosny Aîné. *Helgvor of the Blue River; The Givreuse Enigma; The Mysterious Force; The Navigators of Space; Vamireh; The World of the Variants; The Young Vampire*

Marcel Rouff. *Journey to the Inverted World*

Marie-Anne de Roumier-Robert. *The Voyage of Lord Seaton to the Seven Planets*

Léonie Rouzade. *The World Turned Upside Down*

Han Ryner. *The Human Ant; The Superhumans*

Louis-Claude de Saint-Martin. *The Crocodile*

Frank Schildiner. *The Quest of Frankenstein*

Pierre de Selenes: *An Unknown World*

Norbert Sevestre. *Sâr Dubnotal: Vs. Jack the Ripper; The Astral Trail*

Angelo de Sorr. *The Vampires of London*

Brian Stableford. *The Empire of the Necromancers (1. The Shadow of Frankenstein; 2. Frankenstein and the Vampire Countess; 3. Frankenstein in London); Eurydice's Lament; The New Faust at the Tragicomique; Sherlock Holmes and The Vampires of Eternity; The Stones of Camelot; The Wayward Muse.* (anthologist) *News from the Moon; The Germans on Venus; The Supreme Progress; The World Above the World; Nemoville; Investigations of the Future; The Conqueror of Death; The Revolt of the Machines; The Man With the Blue Face; The Aerial Valley; The New Moon; The Nickel Man; On the Brink of the World's End; The Mirror of Present Events; The Humanishere*

Jacques Spitz. *The Eye of Purgatory*

Kurt Steiner. *Ortog*

Eugène Thébault. *Radio-Terror*

C.-F. Tiphaigne de La Roche. *Amilec*

Simon Tyssot de Patot. *The Strange Voyages of Jacques Massé and Pierre de Mésange*

Louis Ulbach. *Prince Bonifacio*

Théo Varlet. *The Castaways of Eros; The Golden Rock.; The Martian Epic* (w/Octave Joncquel); *Timeslip Troopers* (w/André Blandin); *The Xenobiotic Invasion*
Pierre Véron. *The Merchants of Health*
Paul Vibert. *The Mysterious Fluid*
Villiers de l'Isle-Adam. *The Scaffold; The Vampire Soul*
Gaston de Wailly. *The Murderer of the World*
Philippe Ward. *Artahe; Manhattan Ghost* (w/Mickael Laguerre); *The Song of Montségur* (w/Sylvie Miller)

Victor Margueritte. *The Bacheloress; The Companion; The Couple*

NON-FICTION

Stephen R. Bissette. *Blur 1-5. Green Mountain Cinema 1; Teen Angels*
Win Scott Eckert. *Crossovers* (2 vols.)
Georges Grison. *The Heads that Fell in Paris*
Jean-Marc & Randy Lofficier. *Shadowmen* (2 vols.)
Randy Lofficier. *Over Here*
Brian Stableford. *The Plurality of Imaginary Worlds*

CPSIA information can be obtained
at www.ICGtesting.com
Printed in the USA
FSOW01n0922110916
24872FS